Chan, Tea, and the Way of the Warrior

Jesse J. Berry

Publisher: **Tea Warrior Publishing**
ISBN: **0692263454**
ISBN 13: **978-0692263457**
Library of Congress Control Number: **2014947016**
Tea Warrior Publishing, Greenville, OH

To my oldest daughter, Violet, my closest kung fu confidante and fellow writer; and my other children, Kendall, Katelynn, and Avery—nothing motivates a person more than being a parent. To my wife, Kim, who supports everything I do, no matter how crazy. To my sipai, especially my sifu, Master Chango Noaks. Though we are on different paths now, I owe a great deal of who I am to him. Finally, to Amanda Williams, my dear friend and fellow author. Thanks for all the great help and insight.

Acknowledgments

I would like to thank the following individuals for supporting me in my efforts to make this novel possible. It could not have been done without them.

Adetokunbo Adeshile, Allen Hartman, Chad Garrett, Chris Langdon, Jay Roberts II, Justin Berry, Ronald Berry Jr., Seth Hughes, Tyler Penny, and the Williams family—Claire (extra thanks for your insight), Rob, Ash, and Leo.

And anyone else who helped make this publication possible. You know who you are.

one

Abandon all hope all ye who enter here.
—Dante Alighieri

Suuuuuck...suuuuuck...suuuuuck...suuuuuck...suuuuuck...suuuuuck...
Elliot stared at the featherless ass of every dead turkey that passed by. The turkeys were headless by the time they got to Elliot, so he didn't have to look into their vacant eyes—just the big puckered asses staring up at him. He shoved a one-inch-diameter vacuum tube into the ass of each Meleagris, sucking as much feces out as he could in the few moments he shared with them. This was to prevent feces from running out all over the carcass or onto other workers during further processing.

The processing plant was dank, poorly lit, and very loud. It was so loud that there was a state regulation requiring every employee to wear hearing protection. The loudest noise came from the overhead mechanical track that held the hangers from which the turkeys hung. A few people, such as Elliot and Steve, the next guy down the line, had air tools. Steve had an air-powered circular rotating blade much like a hole saw, except instead of teeth on the blade, it had a razor edge. And in the center, instead of a drill, it had a short, thin metal guide rod. Steve would stick the guide rod into the turkey's anal canal while the blade cut out the anus. The real skill was to not cut too deep and sever the anal canal or any other part of the rectum, which would make it harder for the pullers to reach in and remove all of the innards. Not to mention the excess mess it made.

In addition to the noise of the pneumatic tools, there was a fast-flowing canal in the floor, just behind the processing line. It was exceptionally loud for how small and shallow it was. This creek was where the pullers, who were farther down the line from Elliot, threw the innards to be carried away to God knows where.

There were the constant indistinguishable noises from up and down the processing line and other parts of the plant, painfully harmonizing to the rhythm of Elliot's continuously sucking vacuum. However, for Elliot, the loudest and most distinguishable noise was the ticking of the clock, which he could always hear, even over the loudest cacophony of industrial noises. It ticked away, growing louder with each passing second. *Oh God...I'm not going to look at the clock. I'm not going to look at the clock.*

But the ticking would grow louder...louder...Elliot could swear that the ticks were slowing down as they grew more deafening. Soon, the sharp ticks gave way to a more hollow sound, a sound reminiscent of the wood blocks from elementary-school music class. Everyone liked to play the wood blocks, Elliot remembered, because it was easy, and everyone liked to hit them unnecessarily hard. The sound was just like the pounding of the clock that was calling out to Elliot, "Look at me! Look what time I show!"

Elliot would look around to see if anyone else heard the slow, steady boom of the clock beating louder and louder, thinking that someone else had to hear it, but no one did. Elliot would sometimes close his eyes tight and think, *I'm not going to look. Don't look.* But eventually he would give in, and, with a heavy sigh, he would say out loud, "Damn it! It's only been..." He was often surprised at his own outbursts and would nervously look around to see if anyone had noticed, but no one ever did. Today, he looked up and thought, *Only forty minutes into the day,* and then he let out another long sigh.

Suuuuuck...suuuuuck...suuuuuck...suuuuuck...suuuuuck... suuuuuck...

Elliot shifted his weight from one leg to another, standing in the same spot he had stood in every day for the past two years—eight, ten, sometimes twelve hours a day—doing the same job, sucking shit out of a dead turkey's ass. His body ached from standing there for so long, and he often wondered how much he'd contributed to the concave worn into the floor from generations of workers standing in that exact spot.

It was very cold inside the processing plant. This was to keep the meat from spoiling. Elliot wore a hairnet, a hard hat, safety glasses, a sweatshirt, a heavy plastic apron, rubber gloves that went to his elbows, jeans, and heavy-duty, steel-toed, rubber, knee-high boots, all of which hung loosely from his scrawny frame. Still, the dampness penetrated all of his armor and seeped into his body. Throughout the line, there were a couple of stations where blood, feces, puke, and semi digested grain would spray out during the mutilation of the turkeys. Water from all of the processing stations, along with bodily fluids, would run off of the dead birds and onto the workers, onto the floor, and down into the river of death. All of that running water and gore everywhere made it unbearably damp.

Every once in a while, Elliot would shiver and shudder at the wetness and remember his first week at the processing plant as a puller. After shit was sucked from the fowl's ass, the anus was cut out and hung to the side. Then, the V cutter would slice from the new anal opening up the inner crease of both thighs, making a V-shaped opening big enough to get a hand in. A puller would stick his hand as far inside the carcass as he could and try to get a hold of every organ so as to yank everything out in one attempt. The hardest organ to get was the heart. It was so far up and so soft and squishy that it easily slipped through the fingers. Sometimes the puller wouldn't even notice he missed it. Pulling was the only job on the line that took skill, however little, besides boning. But boning took a lot of seniority, which Elliot did not have, so he never considered applying for boning jobs.

Elliot started out as a puller and caught on very quickly, but the other pullers did not care for Elliot, and he didn't care much for them. The pullers were always talking bad about other coworkers when they weren't around, but acted very friendly to them when they were. They also talked very crudely about women. Although Elliot was indifferent to most of what the pullers said, he didn't like saying those kinds of things and didn't share his coworkers' opinions. Sometimes, though, when one of them would make a remark to Elliot, he would want to make a crude remark of his own, just to fit in, but couldn't think of any or couldn't bring himself to do it. This always created an awkward moment. He knew it wouldn't be long before he would be moved to some other undesirable job. It was the same everywhere he worked. He was always quiet, awkward, and no fun, so he would eventually be moved to some shitty job that no one wanted. Only this time, it was, literally, a shitty job. This job was so terrible that they usually rotated people every couple of days so no one person would have to suffer too long. But Elliot's bosses didn't care for him either, and after a while, despite what a good puller he was, they put him on the vacuum.

Suuuuuck...suuuuuck...suuuuuck...suuuuuck...suuuuuck... suuuuuck...

Elliot shivered again and thought back to pulling, remembering how he'd had to stick his hand so far into the carcass that even his elbow-length rubber gloves would be enveloped and fill with blood, puke, feces, and gore, soaking the cotton gloves he wore on the inside for padding and warmth. It was a disgusting job. In his first couple of days, he thought he was not going to hack it, especially when some of the bodily fluids shot into his face. He was not required to wear a face shield, and no one else did, so, against his real desire to wear one, he chose not to.

Really, it was the smell that was the hardest to get over; even now, two years later, Elliot still struggled with it. The stench of feces, puke, and death could be smelled for miles and miles around. Every day, his clothes would be doused with the nasty concoction of bodily fluids, and he would carry the rancid smell of industrial animal processing home with him, stinking up his tiny apartment. It was so strong that his neighbor Drew could sometimes smell it through the walls. Drew would pound on the wall and yell profanities: "What the fuck, Elliot? You smell like ass...literally! Take a shower, burn your clothes, *move to another apartment!*" Although being a puller was wetter and covered him from head to toe in gore and odor, Elliot still wished they had let him stay a puller.

Suddenly, Elliot could hear laughing and jeers from some of his coworkers farther up the line, and he waited for the inevitable: half of a skinned neck shoved partway into a turkey's ass. His coworkers thought the skinned neck looked like a giant skinned penis, and they were always sending them to him in the turkeys' anuses or hiding them in his locker. Sometimes one would mysteriously hit him when he wasn't looking. Usually, these incidents came with homosexual jokes or innuendos. Elliot could never figure out why, everywhere he worked, everyone would make fun of him for being gay, even though he was not. *Maybe it's not that they think I'm gay, it's just that they're not creative enough to think of better insults. Or maybe they're all obsessed with homosexuality because, deep down, they're homosexuals,* he would think to himself. He always wanted to say that to them, but he was too afraid. Elliot liked to think that he was just ignoring the constant jokes and insults and that he was a better person for not retaliating. But, deep down, he knew it was fear.

"Well, well, it looks like sissy boy is molest'n defenseless animals again." Elliot didn't even have to look to know that it was Marvin. Marvin harassed Elliot the most and was the principal instigator in most of the ridicule and humiliation aimed at him. Elliot wasn't sure what job Marvin did, but somehow, Marvin got to walk around a lot and talk to people, which meant that he had ample opportunity to torment others. Elliot always noticed the belt of knives and the sharpening steel that Marvin wore around his waist, but he could not guess exactly what cutting job there was that didn't require the man to stay at his workstation. Everyone liked Marvin, and Elliot could not figure that out either.

Marvin seemed taller than he was because of his long, lanky limbs. Elliot hated everything about Marvin, including his long, dirty, black hair that refused to completely stay in his hairnet. And no one would ever make the man correct the problem. The few errant strands of hair always appeared greasy and seemed to stick to his unshaven face. His facial hair was long enough to require a beard net but not thick enough to be a full beard. Like the strands of loose hair, no one ever made Marvin wear a beard net, and that was something else that irritated Elliot.

Marvin was always laughing and joking with everyone, and Elliot didn't see why everyone thought he was funny. Marvin was not witty, and his jokes were repetitive and bland. All of the taunts and insults he made about others were the same, including the ones to and about Elliot. All of them were jokes about the other person being gay or girly, and to Elliot, they weren't even good jokes. *Is everyone else as stupid as he is?* Elliot would think to himself.

Even though Elliot made no reply and showed no emotion, Marvin continued: "Uh-oh! Baby's going to cry?"

My life is just grade school repeating itself over and over again, Elliot thought.

"Good thing we got Elliot's tear trough to catch all those tears!" another coworker called out.

Yeah, good one, Elliot thought before letting out yet another long sigh.

"What the fuck is this? Elliot, if you're going to do that kind of gay shit, keep it at home," Steve shouted loudly enough for everyone, including George, Elliot's immediate supervisor, to hear. Then Steve pulled the severed neck out of the turkey's ass and threw it at Elliot's feet. Elliot was too focused on trying to ignore Marvin and his other coworkers to notice George walk up behind him.

"Goddamn it, Elliot! We don't put up with that kinda shit here. We have a don't-ask-don't-tell policy! Ya wanna do sick things, you go to the store and buy your own turkey, and do it in the privacy of your own home! *And stop interfering with work*! You're makin' it harder for everyone else t' do their job!"

Marvin had casually walked away, laughing with everyone else, as George walked up and shouted his reprimand. George stood behind Elliot for several more minutes before walking away. Everyone went back to his or her own thoughts, and Elliot went back to his feeble attempts to ignore the cold, damp smell of the place and the clock that continued to tattoo his brain with every pounding tick. With a long, silent sigh, Elliot thought, *Oh God, I can't look up. Don't look up.*

* * *

At the end of the day, as Elliot was lacing up his shoes in the locker room, a couple of guys who worked down at the farther end of the line came in.

"How's it going?" one of them asked.

"Good, now that it's over," the other replied.

How cliché, Elliot thought. Everyone greeted and replied to each other in the same way, with only slight variation. If it had been earlier in the day, the conversation would have sounded more like this:

"How's it going?"

"It'll be better when I get outta here."

Then there was the ever-classic "Same shit, different day." Elliot hated this statement most—if not for its excessive use, for its reference to shit, something that Elliot did not want to be reminded of.

Elliot noted that some people had their own catchphrases or stock replies. A line worker who pulled fat off the flaps that hung loosely around the holes that the V cutters made always said, "Just another wonderful day," as sarcastically as he could every time someone asked, "How's it going?" In fact, Elliot recalled plenty of times when this worker would even greet people by saying, "Just another wonderful day."

There was another guy who would always reply to "How's it going?" with "As well as can be expected in this place." Whenever Elliot thought about all of the repetitive things his coworkers said, and then tried to imagine how he would respond, he could never think of anything better. It didn't matter much, because no one ever asked him how his day was or how he was doing.

When Elliot got into his car, he let out a long, deliberate sigh. *God, why?* He did not believe in God in the Christian sense and questioned the existence of God in any terms, but as much as he questioned, as much as he tried not to believe, he constantly called out to God. As always, when he thought about God, he couldn't help but think about Briseis. She was a believer, and thoughts on God inevitably led back to her. Elliot began to wonder where she was and what she was doing but then stopped himself, knowing that thinking about her made him feel bad—or worse. Elliot quickly thought about tea and wanted desperately to get home, get cleaned up, and go to the tea salon.

After getting home and cleaning up, Elliot made the long drive through run-down neighborhoods to WabiCha Teahouse on the other side of town. WabiCha was located in a small shopping district near a large community college. The shopping district, populated with middle-class college kids, seemed out of place in the midst of lower-class urban sprawl.

On the drive to WabiCha, Elliot reflected back to a couple of months ago, when he had first met Chin Li, the owner. It was about six months prior to meeting the owner that he had discovered the tiny salon while out for a walk. Elliot, a long-practicing tea drinker, had never heard of WabiCha. The only other teahouse in town was High Tea, a classy English teahouse that didn't serve the Chinese or Japanese teas Elliot was partial to. In contrast to WabiCha, High Tea was located in an upscale shopping district between two wealthy neighborhoods and near a very high-end shopping mall. Elliot did not care for English teas and felt very uncomfortable in the highbrow establishment full of yuppies, fancy tea sets, and very expensive menu.

Despite how out of place he felt, Elliot loved tea so much and wanted to like English teas so badly that he visited High Tea twice. And though the servers had been friendly, Elliot was certain, or at least suspect, that he had detected subtle hints of contempt. The last time he went there, he had thought about the name High Tea and wondered if the owners were aware of the irony of the name and their establishment. Traditionally, high tea was a pastime of working-class commoners when they returned home for dinner in the evenings after a long day of work—the "high time" of the day. It was simply tea that they drank with their meals, not some fancy ceremony like low tea, which was the morning or midday tea of the aristocracy.

Elliot was very happy to find that WabiCha Teahouse had very traditional, simple Chinese decor and an extensive tea menu. The salon was quaint, with a very small seating area of only six small, dark, wood-stained square tables. The lights were always very low and the conversations quiet, creating a calming atmosphere. The few servers were young, attractive Asian females, who Elliot thought contributed to the aesthetic appeal. The mysterious tea-shop owner, who would sit in the back room and rarely come out, always intrigued Elliot, making WabiCha Teahouse even more compelling.

The day Elliot and the salon owner met, Elliot had been reading *Hagakure: The Book of the Samurai*, a book he had recently started. The owner had spoken to him from behind and, in a heavy Chinese accent, said, "Ah, *Book of Hidden Leaves*," calling it by its rarely used translation. Elliot had turned, and before he had gotten a chance to say anything, the old man had continued: "A must 'ead fo' any adept student of wa'." Elliot had just sat there, looking stupefied, before the shop owner had spoken further, "I knew you we'e wa'io' fi'st day I see you in my shop. My name Chin Li."

Elliot had been completely shocked at the old man's surprising introduction and compliment. Although Chin Li showed no signs of mockery, Elliot could not help but feel somewhat defensive. Calling someone a warrior was not a compliment used in this day and age, and it made Elliot feel very awkward. He often imagined being a warrior in some other time, in some other culture, and felt that being considered a warrior would be the greatest compliment anyone could give him. All he could do was stutter, "Uhhh, I'm Elliot."

Chin Li was old and had long gray hair that hung past his shoulders and that he kept in a well-groomed ponytail. He reminded Elliot of the old shopkeeper from the '80s movie *Gremlins.* But the old man's mannerisms reminded Elliot of Mr. Miyagi, the karate master from another popular '80s movie, *The Karate Kid.* "So it is young Maste' Elliot. Pleasu'e to meet you." And the old man gave a slight but distinct bow.

"Uh, pleasure to meet you...uh, Master Chin...Li," replied Elliot in a questioning tone, as if asking if that was the correct thing to say. Then Elliot returned the bow.

"Ha-ha, please, please call me Li." The old man's laugh reminded Elliot of the way old masters chuckled in old kung fu films with bad overdubbing.

In that first conversation, Chin Li had asked, "What you do fo' living?" and "What ma'tial a't you do?" Everything about the mysterious old man—his sudden introduction and the fact that he had guessed Elliot trained in martial arts—surprised Elliot. Elliot was embarrassed to tell Chin Li about his work. To Elliot, working in a factory was not a respectable career, and on the rare occasion that he told someone about his work, he could almost see the person's respect, if there had been any to begin with, melt away. But he didn't know what else to say, and despite his fear that Chin Li would also lose respect for him, he told the wise old tea-shop owner about his work, about the kung fu he trained in, and who his sifu was. Chin Li did not allude to knowing Elliot's sifu or being familiar with his kung fu. The kind old man just responded with polite affirmations, listening sincerely. Chin Li never had the look of boredom or contempt that Elliot was used to receiving. However, Elliot was afraid that Chin Li was just hiding his contempt behind common courtesy, and in Elliot's panic, he had cut the conversation short. "Uh, well, I really have to get going. It was nice meeting you."

Having regretted cutting that first conversation with the charismatic shop owner short, Elliot tried to think of a reason to approach the old man and strike up another conversation, but he could never come up with one. So he would go to the tea salon and hope that the old man would approach him. Now, on his way to WabiCha Teahouse, he tried extra hard to think of a reason to talk to Chin Li, but despite his best efforts, he could still think of nothing. So, as usual, he sat in the tea salon, pretending to read while slowly drinking his tea and occasionally stealing glances toward the back, desperately hoping to see Chin Li emerging from the back room to come and talk to him. But to Elliot's dismay, the old shop owner never approached.

* * *

Elliot wriggled and flailed his arms, trying to defend himself against the oncoming barrage of punches that his sih-ing, Austin Horvath, rained down upon him. Throughout the sparring match Sifu Miller was yelling instructions to Elliot: "Get your hips outta there!" and "Snake out! Snake out!" and

"Keep swimming—stay busy!" But Elliot could not free himself from the inferior position he was in. Although it was heavy-to-full contact, the larger, older man was not hitting Elliot very hard from his top-mount position. But the onslaught of strikes down upon Elliot overwhelmed his sense of security and broke him down into a complete panic. This heavy-to-full-contact conditioning was an integral part of Elliot's kung fu training. He had been learning kung fu under Sifu Miller for nearly two years. Sifu Miller insisted that a person could not master martial arts by simply learning the techniques and drills but had to experience combat in real time.

"Experience is the best teacher. A fighter with no official training, but actual fighting experience, will always beat the master who has never fought or competed," Sifu Miller would often say. Elliot never liked sparring class. The mere thought of it brought on anxiety that would almost make him sick. It was not uncommon for Elliot to miss class because of this feeling. Even the classes that focused more on drills, techniques, and concepts—the how and why—and less on physical conditioning filled Elliot with dread. However, nothing compared to the anxiety he felt while sparring. A lot of this apprehension was because he struggled to understand the sophisticated principles and concepts and felt he couldn't acquire the skills necessary for applying the techniques. He often asked himself why he even went to kung fu, and he spent most of his days wrestling with an almost overwhelming desire to quit.

Elliot had met Sifu Miller at a bookstore while browsing through the history section. The kung fu teacher was middle-aged and of average size, with no distinguishable features. His brown hair was cut into a subtle military style, his eyes were grayish blue and soft, and his clothes were ordinary, though he wore a hooded sweatshirt that said "Shaolin Academy" across the front. The man did not strike Elliot as a martial arts master.

Sifu Miller saw Elliot flipping through a copy of *Thucydides* and struck up a conversation. Sifu Miller was very charismatic, and Elliot, like everyone else, loved him immediately. They chatted for nearly an hour about different warrior societies and histories, and Sifu Miller told Elliot all about kung fu and its history. The idea of training to be a warrior greatly appealed to Elliot. Elliot had long studied history, especially warrior societies, and dreamed of a better time and better place.

Shortly after meeting Sifu Miller, Elliot went to try some classes and had been Sifu Miller's student ever since. However, his anxiety toward training constantly called his conviction into question—a question he often struggled to answer. On a subconscious level, the only thing that outweighed his anxiety for returning to class was Sifu Miller. Sifu Miller was the only male role model Elliot had ever had.

"Relax! You gotta stay relaxed," Sifu Miller was shouting. But Elliot could never relax; he was tense and stiff even before the match started. And as soon as Sifu Miller said, "Go," his whole body stiffened even more. This tension was very taxing on Elliot's quickly deteriorating energy and caused him to become exhausted and "gas out" right away— sometimes before the match even started. His tension also made it hard for him to move efficiently and effectively. It made his strikes slow and predictable, and it was easy for his opponents to out strike him or grapple and throw him.

By the end of sparring, Elliot felt sick and worn out by excessive heavy breathing and being beaten on the head and body, along with the usual anxiety that training brought on. But most of all, he was sick from embarrassment. Elliot always felt he was the worst student, and he was sure everyone else knew it. No one ever said anything, but Elliot was certain the other students talked about him behind his back. *How can they not? Even the new students and the young students are tougher and better than me,* he would often think to himself before letting out a sigh.

Once the match was over, Sihing Horvath helped Elliot up, and the two men bowed to each other and then to Sifu, as was proper etiquette. Sifu Miller then lined up all of the students and bowed everyone out. Shaolin Academy was a small school with a long, narrow floor space that barely held the thirteen students present for class. The face of the school was an old storefront window that made up the entire front of Shaolin Academy's space. Aside from a door that led to the office, restroom, and basement locker room stairs in the back, the training space was open and empty, with worn-out, old blue mats covering the training floor. Old mirrors lined one wall of the training area, and countless layers of old, chipped white paint covered the other. The lighting was surprisingly bright, considering how old the fluorescent lights and drop ceiling looked. The school felt dank and humid, and steam rolled down all of the glass surfaces, as it always did after a night of training.

After class, Elliot changed his clothes while everyone else laughed and joked, discussing their matches and training with one another. No one said good-bye as Elliot left the tiny basement locker room, which felt crowded due to the four other students and very poor lighting. Just at the top of the basement steps was the office, and on his way by, Elliot stopped and looked in. The office was also very small, with barely enough room for a desk and chair and two folding chairs sitting in front of the desk. There were several old certificates of completion hanging on the wall. The opened mail and old invoices on the desk, a trash can full of discarded papers, and a lot of accumulated dust made the office seem surprisingly empty despite how small it was; it was clear that Sifu Miller, or anyone else, spent very little time in there.

Sifu Miller was explaining the four conditions of superior facing an opponent to Austin Horvath, the most senior student, and a newer student. "You have inside closed stance, called *ji ng ma tiu*. You have outside closed stance, called *ji ng ma buht*. You have inside open stance, called *bin ma tiu*. And you have outside open stance, called *bin ma buht*. By understanding these angles, you will be able to establish superior position, and by understanding bridging—knowing which weapon to use at what range—you'll be able to establish superior time. With superior time and space, you'll always be able to hit your target while leaving no target for your opponent. Time is distance, and space is position..." Sifu Miller looked between Austin and the other student and noticed Elliot.

Before the teacher could say anything, Elliot said, "Good night, sir. Good night, sihing, sidai," and gave a bow to each one in turn.

The two students half turned to Elliot, returned the bow, and said good night. Sifu Miller, seeming surprised that Elliot was leaving, also bowed and said, "Oh, good night, sir," and immediately went back to talking with the two students. Elliot walked out into the empty street of the once-bustling district. This district had once had a culture all its own, with tiny art galleries, theaters, coffee bars, independent record shops, and venues catering to a generation of hipsters and cut off from the rest of the world. Now all that remained were run-down old buildings with boarded windows—a city lost.

Elliot walked down the dark street under a flickering lamp-post and past the trash that blew like tumbleweeds across his path. The image reminded him of a scene from a melo-dramatic movie, and he wondered about the irony of his life.

When Elliot got home, he felt exceptionally worn out from training. He wanted desperately to get to sleep, but a voice inside his head kept reminding him that he didn't sleep very well. *Damn it! I'm so tired. I know I'm not going to be able to sleep. Just one night. Just one fucking night!* But as soon as he closed his eyes, his alarm went off, and he felt as if he hadn't slept at all.

two

No one saves us but ourselves.
—Buddha

The days and weeks seemed to blur together for Elliot. He
had been feeling exceptionally lonely. For years, he'd tried
to convince himself that he didn't need anyone. This concept
of not needing anyone was what had attracted him to warrior cultures and lifestyles. Everything Elliot had ever learned
about the lone warrior and his detachment from worldly
things and relationships had motivated Elliot to adopt the
same mind-set. He had studied warrior philosophy extensively in an attempt to understand how an individual can
live a life of solitude amid society. But despite his extensive
study and best efforts, he had failed to convince himself that
he needed no one.

Elliot drifted through the day in a state of semi consciousness. It was as if he were being woken from a long sleep
when he finally heard Sifu Miller repeat, "How are you feeling
these days, Elliot? You seem a little down lately. Is everything all right?"

Elliot did not know how to respond to his sifu's inquiry.
Sifu Miller asked this question every once in a while, but it
always seemed as if the teacher asked simply as a courtesy.

This time was different. His sifu just sat there and stared, waiting for a response. Elliot knew he was not going to be bought off with a simple, "Good, Sifu, thank you." Suddenly, he wanted to open up and confess, tell his sifu about his feelings, but he couldn't. He felt ashamed of his depression and thought it made him weak.

Sifu Miller seemed to detect that Elliot was uncomfortable with the question by Elliot's half-shrugging response and the stuttered sounds of "Uh...OK."

Sifu Miller shifted the subject and asked, "How's work?"

At this question, Elliot could think of a response but didn't want to say it out loud. The mere thought or utterance of work flooded Elliot with anxiety. He tried to quickly think of an empty reply that would end the conversation. His mind was filled with the cliché replies he heard so often that they burned in his ears and deadened his heart. They were driven into his head, day after day and year after year, and now they were trying to get out. Taking in a deep breath and letting it out slowly, Elliot hopelessly searched for something else to say—anything—but to his dismay, he blurted out, "Same old, same old, I guess."

After a short pause, Sifu Miller continued. "You've told me a little about your job before, but I haven't really heard you talk much about it since."

"Well, there's not much to talk about, really. I stand in the same exact spot, day in and day out, doing the same exact menial task over and over again, day in and day out. And I work with a bunch of..." Elliot paused for a moment, suddenly afraid that he was about to breach etiquette by cursing and speaking disrespectfully of others, but he could not completely stop himself. "Jerks," he continued, "including my boss. There's not much to talk about."

Elliot was surprised at how much he'd said and how quickly he'd responded. There was subtle but distinct defensiveness in his reply. His tone even had a hint of hostility. And though the unexpected and sudden change in his mood surprised Elliot, it was his unfamiliarity with these emotions that really confused him. As confusion washed away the sudden anger, Elliot wondered why he would react that way to begin with. He had never reacted or acted that way before and didn't even know that he was capable of such an attitude. Nor could he figure out why he would act that way toward his sifu. His teacher had only asked about work. There were no insinuations or indications of a malicious motive in his inquiry.

A slight smile slowly grew across Sifu Miller's face. It was warm and understanding. "You know, Elliot, work would not be so bad if you didn't resist it so much."

Elliot could feel the hostility start to rise again, and again he wondered about the foreign emotion and where it was coming from. He could not remember a time when he had felt anger or hostility, only the idea of it. He took a deep breath and forced himself to relax.

Sifu Miller went on. "You know, in here, we study Chan and its Taoist influence. Well...Taoism is the path of least resistance. You must harmonize. I know I say that all the time out on the floor, practicing techniques, but that is a concept that applies to everyday living."

Elliot wasn't sure he understood his sifu or where he was going with this statement, so he just frowned slightly and gave a little nod. Sifu Miller ignored the frown and continued. "You have to love your job. Make it something you love. If you do that, then it won't be bad. Why would you suffer doing something you love? You have to want to like it. You *have* to want it. If you love your job, you rob those who try and make you miserable of the power to do so. No one makes you hate your job. *You* choose to hate it, just like *you* can choose to love it."

Elliot knew that his sifu was alluding to self-control, but he didn't want to hear it. In a slightly more defensive tone, Elliot said, "But, Sifu, there's nothing to love about it. I stand there all day, sticking a vacuum in a turkey's...in, uh..." Again he paused out of fear of breaching etiquette and speaking inappropriately, but he was unable to stop himself. "In a turkey's ass. I'm sorry, but there's no better way to say it."

"OK. It's OK. I understand it's not glamorous work—"

"Sifu, you *don't* understand. I've heard you give this lecture before. You talk about loving even the things you hate and how you have to take pride in them...that pride is what ultimately makes you love the job. But there's no pride in what I do. I take no ownership or responsibility in the end product. The quality of the end product is going to be the same no matter how well I do my job. I could stop doing my job and it would not affect the end product. That turkey is going to come out the same way no matter what. I would have to try hard to mess that job up. I could literally do that job blindfolded. How do I take pride in something that takes absolutely no skill? If I had to butcher, clean, and strip the turkey myself, I could see taking pride in something like that. The skill it would take and being responsible for the end product, the quality of it. But I don't. I do one measly step, the most unimportant step—one that could easily be left out of the process. Where is there pride in that?"

Sifu Miller sat silently, looking down, nodding his head ever so slightly while processing Elliot's response. "You have to find the positive in everything, even in a job you view as pointless. You stand there all day, thinking about how meaningless your job is, how much you hate it, and sometimes wondering why you're even there..."

Now Elliot was looking down and nodding his head in agreement, slightly embarrassed at his outburst. Sifu Miller continued, "You probably forget why you even work there sometimes. You spend all day thinking about the negative. I want you to think about the positive. Don't think about the one simple step you're responsible for or how meaningless you think it is. Think about how hard it is to stand there all day and do it. You say that it is so easy that anyone can do it? That may be true, but can anyone do it for as long as you can? Have you asked your bosses or coworkers what the turnover rate is for that particular job? That is what you should be taking pride in. The fact you have the will to do that job for as long as it takes without complaint. And doing it with coworkers who treat you badly and bosses who don't appreciate you takes even more strength and fortitude. Not many people could handle that situation and environment. In fact, what you tolerate on a daily basis is the essence of what it is to be a warrior—that constant struggle, conquering yourself, overcoming your negativity, and forcing yourself to have a positive outlook."

Elliot scoffed a little at these words, but deep down, he did feel a little bit of pride. He had never thought of it that way. Sifu Miller was right: not many people could tolerate that job for as long as he had, especially with his coworkers. He knew his coworkers couldn't handle his job or being ridiculed day in and day out the way he did. The more he thought about it, the more pride he felt. This pride was also a new feeling for Elliot, and suddenly it scared him. The pride quickly gave way to a flood of more embarrassment that he tried very hard to hide.

"You also have to think about what you have that is a result of your work. You know, you're a student, always reading and learning; you come here for learning, and none of it's free. Books and kung fu training cost money, and I can't forget tea. I know how much you love tea, and I know how expensive it gets. So instead of thinking about the negative things your job brings, think about the positive. Force yourself to maintain a positive outlook. That's the inner struggle. That's conquering one's self."

Elliot already knew what his sifu was going to say next before he said it. He said it over and over in training to drill it into the students' heads. It was the difference between a warrior and a fighter. "And you know that a warrior conquers himself. Fighters...they conquer others. You're a warrior, and your coworkers are fighters, trying to conquer you through intimidation and humiliation."

Elliot continued to sit in silence, contemplating what his sifu was saying. He didn't totally get it, but he understood enough. Then, Sifu Miller went on. "You just have to accept them for who they are. You can't let them get to you. *Do not let them conquer you. You* conquer you."

Sifu Miller didn't actually know Elliot's coworkers or how they treated him, so the mere suggestion of accepting them offended Elliot, and he felt that hostility rise yet again. Without resisting the urge, he responded, "How can you ask me to accept them? They're...assholes! Tolerating them is one thing, but accepting them, I mean..."

Elliot could feel the hostility growing stronger inside him, and he could not control it anymore. The angrier he got, the more confused he became at the strange new emotion. He did not want to argue or be rude to his sifu, and he knew it was bad etiquette to question his teacher, but he couldn't fathom accepting his coworkers—his enemies. That was just too much. Elliot felt that he could try to change his attitude about his job and try to "conquer himself," but accepting his coworkers...

Sifu Miller could see that Elliot was having a hard time with this concept. "Elliot, do you know the Buddhist parable about the frogs and the alligator?"

Elliot was looking down into his lap and shook his head without looking up. Sifu Miller went on. "A frog hopped up to the bank of a rushing river, wanting to cross to the other side. But the river was too fast, and the frog was afraid of being carried away. While he looked across to the other side, an alligator stuck his head up out of the water and said, 'Frog, you look like you wish to cross to the other side. Do not be afraid of the fast current. Climb on my back, and I will ferry you across.' Halfway across, the alligator ate the frog. Well, another frog came to the same spot, wanting to cross the river, but was also afraid of the rushing water. Again, the alligator stuck his head up and said, 'Frog, I see you wish to cross the mad river. Do not be afraid of the rushing water. I will ferry you across.'

"The frog replied, 'Alligator, you ate the last frog that rode on your back. I do not want to be eaten.'

"'You are right, but I am full now. Do not worry; I will ferry you across safely,' responded the alligator. But halfway across, the alligator ate the frog.

"Finally, a third frog approached the bank, and when the alligator stuck his head out of the water, the frog asked, 'Alligator, why did you eat those frogs?'

"The alligator said, 'Because I'm an alligator.' So you see, Elliot, you can't hate something for what it is."

They both fell silent again. Elliot was no longer angry. His sifu was right, and he knew it. His coworkers were alligators, and he was a frog. *Maybe Sifu is right. Maybe if I don't spend all day thinking about how much I hate work, it won't be so bad. And my coworkers, those people, Marvin! Maybe if I just let them have their fun...not care...*

"You know, in the children's class, I talk all the time about self-control and what it means. Do you know?"

Elliot knew his sifu would come back to self-control. He had heard him lecture on self-control countless times and felt silly having to answer, knowing that his sifu knew that he knew the answer. "Uh, yeah...self-control is when I control my body and emotions."

"Yes! Body *and* emotions. We choose to be happy or sad or angry. Sometimes, when we're not paying attention, we run into a door or something, or we trip or somehow hurt ourselves, and we are immediately frustrated. Right there, we choose to either stay mad or...or...we choose not to let it ruin our day. Most people will stay in a bad mood. What would you do? Would you have the willpower and self-control to say, 'I'm not going to let this ruin my day,' or would you have a bad attitude for the rest of the day?"

Elliot was thinking about what Sifu Miller was saying. Elliot knew that he didn't have to trip or run into a door or anything else to be in a negative mood. He dreaded work so much that he woke up in a bad mood. Sifu Miller went on. "You know, either you control your actions and emotions, or someone or something else will. You let work and your coworkers control your emotions."

They both fell silent again. Sifu Miller was staring at Elliot, and Elliot was looking down at his hands again, too ashamed to make eye contact. The flame that fueled his hostility had flickered out, and he again felt that familiar emotion—shame—for being so weak. *Yes, Sifu is right. I need to control my emotions. I can do this. I can beat work...and those people. Maybe I won't let them get to me anymore.*

After their discussion, Elliot prepared for class and thought about everything his sifu had said. During training, he was distracted by his own thoughts and hopes about his new attitude. He continually imagined how he was going to act at work and how he was going to respond to his coworkers' ridicule.

When Elliot got home that night, he lay in bed and was finally able to focus all of his thoughts on his new determination. The thought of work seemed different—distant and foreign. Elliot imagined that he was preparing for war, and tomorrow was to be the decisive battle. He could not see past tomorrow and felt that, with his newfound willpower and understanding of positive thinking, if he could not go to work tomorrow and win, he was never going to.

* * *

Elliot was startled awake by his alarm clock. He lay in bed thinking about his conversation with his sifu. As he gained full consciousness, he tried to have a positive attitude but could only muster irresoluteness. Sitting up in bed, he tried desperately to block out images of his coworkers. *No! I'm not going to think about them or work at all. I'll cross that bridge when I get there. I'm going to have breakfast and tea and only think about things that make me feel good.* He got up and navigated through the pitch-black darkness of his room, making his way toward the door. But cruel fate tested—or mocked—him, and he kicked the bottom edge of the slightly open door, ripping part of his pinky toenail off.

"Mmmmm...sssssssst. Damn it...damn it! I can't even get out of fucking bed! Of all things—of all fucking things. I... ssssssst..." He thought about the example his sifu had used in their conversation and couldn't believe the irony. Clenching his fist and gritting his teeth, he said out loud for the world to hear, "No! I'm not going to let a stubbed toe ruin my day. This is *my* day! I control my emotions. If I can't take a stubbed toe—or the irony of it—then I have no business..."

He limped to the kitchen to have breakfast and tea and, with much effort, did exactly what he had planned to do: think only about things that made him feel good. When he got to work, he was resolved not to let work or his coworkers get to him. He was determined to not show emotion or exert any energy on their taunts or torments. He was to give them no satisfaction. Fortunately, the day went without incident from his coworkers, but time, however, was relentless. The day wore on and on, and the pounding of the clock seized his very soul with every beat.

Suuuuuck...suuuuuck...suuuuuck...suuuuuck...suuuuuck... suuuuuck...

Thinking back to his chi gung training, Elliot remembered one of his sifu's lectures: "The mind is like a monkey, racing here and there, bouncing around all over the place. You have to tame the monkey."

OK, I can do this. I've got to just clear my mind and think about nothing. I've got to think about nothing. Nothing matters but this moment. I've got to focus on just this moment. And he repeated a verse from *Hagakure* in his head: *"There is nothing other than the single purpose of the present moment. A man's whole life is a succession of moment after moment. If one fully understands the present moment, there will be nothing else to pursue. Live being true to the single purpose of the moment."* Then he ruminated on some of the chi gung techniques that helped focus the mind.

Tick...tick...tick...tick...tick...tick...

But to no avail.

Suuuuuck...suuuuuck...suuuuuck...suuuuuck...suuuuuck... suuuuuck...

Stares from the expired turkeys bore into him. The silent torments of his coworkers hounded him. The clock screamed at him, and time gnawed at him. Today was his day.

three

Nowhere either with more quiet or more freedom from trouble does a man retire than into his own soul, particularly when he has within him such thoughts that by looking into them he is immediately in perfect tranquility.
—Marcus Aurelius

Elliot stared out the window with his book open in front of him, too tired and zoned out to focus. He had long since finished his tea but did not want to go home yet, so he pretended to take a sip from his empty cup, as he so often did. Other times, when Elliot found himself in the predicament of having finished his tea before he wanted to leave, he felt out of place—an overwhelming sense that he didn't belong. He felt as if there were some unspoken law of nature that stated if you were done, you had to go. He watched others to see if they left when they were finished, if they obeyed the natural order, constantly looking for signs of awkwardness and discomfort as the unseen pressures of nature enforced the laws of salons and cafés. But no one ever seemed the least bit uncomfortable. Elliot noticed that people would often sit well beyond his own capacity to stay.

Elliot continued to stare out the front window at the occasional passing car, taking another sip from his empty cup and letting his mind wander to kung fu. As usual, he began to feel guilty about not going to class that evening. Then he hated himself for feeling so guilty all the time about every-thing, like missing a class every once in a while or sitting in the tea salon after he'd finished his tea. *Perhaps I should just buy some more tea.*

Elliot looked down at the tea set and book in front of him and thought, *Ah, tea and reading, the only two pleasures in my life. Tea and reading; I'm such a nerd. No wonder everyone picks on me. 'Picks on me...' Even the way I talk and think is lame.* Correcting himself, he thought, *Gives me shit! Everyone gives me shit!*

He picked up the book and began flipping through the pages, not really stopping on any of them. He began to think about Samurai, Native Americans, Spartans, and other war-rior cultures, as he often would. As his mind went through the usual progression of warrior societies, he inevitably came to the thought of living in one of these societies, picturing him-self a great warrior, striking down anyone who disrespected him. But then negative thoughts would intercede, and, as usual, he would start to wonder, *Would I have even been in the warrior class? Or would I have been a peasant or slave or second-class citizen of some unfortunate type? Or would I have even survived the constant physical trials of some Spartan-type upbringing? Maybe I would have been chucked over the cliff as an infant.*

"Ah, young Maste' Elliot, how a'e you?"

Startled, Elliot turned to see the old shop owner standing with his arms behind his back. Elliot struggled to reply as Chin Li's eyes pierced him.

Even though in their first meeting the shop owner had told Elliot to address him casually, Elliot felt that the old man deserved more respect. He wanted to address the shop owner with the proper etiquette he had learned in kung fu, but he was unsure of the shop owner's title. *Is he a sifu or sensei? Should I call him master or mister?* Elliot stuttered,

"Uh...Mr..." *Is his name Chinli or Chin Li? Does he write it out like an American's, first name and then last? Or like the Chinese, last name first? Is it Mr. Chin or Mr. Li?* "...Chin Li...I'm good. How are you?"

Chin Li chuckled and said, "Ah, please, just Li. Thank you," and gave Elliot a bow.

With an awkward, "Oh, uh, OK...are you sure? I feel like you deserve more than just Li," Elliot returned the bow.

"Please, please, just Li, thank you," he replied and, after a short pause, "Uh, why not t'aining? Is this not t'aining night fo' you?"

"Uh, yeah," Elliot replied with an air of uncertainty, wondering how Chin Li knew he should be at kung fu. His guilt for not going grew; he felt as if he had been caught doing something wrong. "How...how did you know this is the night I train?"

"Ah, so so'y. I neve' see du'ing day and only ce'tain evening—neve' Thu'sday—so I guess you in t'aining Thu'sday. Am I 'ight?"

"Oh, no, it's OK. I mean, I, uh...yeah, you're right. Thursday is one of my nights to train." Elliot was perplexed at Chin Li's observation of his schedule and wondered why he cared enough to take notice. He had only met the intriguing shop owner once. Elliot did not want to admit why he hadn't gone to kung fu, but he could not think of a good reason or excuse fast enough and broke under Chin Li's demanding gaze. "I just had a really long, hard day at work. We've been doing a lot of overtime and stuff, so I thought I'd take the night off," he blurted out.

The old man spoke as if it were of no consequence to him, and his voice even held a hint of understanding. "It is impo'tant to take b'eak. Must get plenty of 'est...and tea. The'e must be balance." Chin Li placed a subtle emphasis on the word tea, grinned slightly, and tilted his head forward a little as if giving another bow.

"I see still 'ead *Book of Leaves*." Chin Li stressed the "l" in *leaves*, struggling to enunciate it correctly. The old man had such a heavy accent that often his "l" sounds were subtle. He dropped his "r" sounds, sometimes replacing the "r" with a hint of a "w" sound. Elliot noticed Chin Li's conscious effort to pronounce this particular word correctly and wondered why.

Continuing to be surprised by the old man, Elliot had forgotten that he was reading the same book, *Hagakure,* that he had been reading the first time he met the shop owner. And again, feeling scrutinized under Chin Li's gaze, he quickly uttered, "Oh, yeah, I was just uh...just, uh, rereading some passages. I've read it before." Elliot didn't want the wise shop owner to think it took him this long to read the book. Elliot feared that the wise tea master would think that Elliot didn't understand it.

Chin Li let out a small chuckle before continuing, "It is good to 'ead books and study, but one should be ca'eful not to study too much. Ve'y bad fo' you. Expe'ience best teache'." And quoting from *Hagakure,* Chin Li said, "'Afte' 'eading book and the like, it best to bu'n them o' th'ow them away. The wo'k of wa'io' is found in ma'tial valo', g'aspping swo'd.'" The old man chuckled again in that old-kung-fu-movie way and said, "It bette' to expe'ience, Maste' Elliot."

Although Elliot had studied *Hagakure* extensively, he was too nervous to catch the slightly paraphrased and heavily accented quote. He also felt as if he had just received a kung fu lesson and was trying very hard to not only commit it to memory but also to think of an intelligent reply. But before he could, Chin Li spoke again. "Is it too late? May I se've you tea? You will do me g'eat hono' if you allow me se've you tea."

Elliot was immediately dumbfounded. He was so shocked at the old man's invitation that he had a hard time processing the request. It was far more than he had ever imagined or hoped for. Elliot had often fantasized about Chin Li coming out and talking to him, but that was it. That was the end of the fantasy. Elliot struggled not to stutter. "Uh...I, uh...it's really getting late. I should...I got work tomorrow...early. I get...uh...I get up early."

But almost before Elliot could get out his last vowel, Chin Li cut in. "Ah, Young Maste' Elliot, there a'e many 'eason not to do something. 'Emembe', expe'ience best teache'. Allow me give you expe'ience."Elliot felt an overwhelming pressure from the tea master, and deep down he really wanted to say yes, but he was nervous—so nervous that he felt himself searching for a way out. But under the constant weight of the old man's stare, he was unable to say no. "Uh, yeah, I'd love it—love that, I mean. It would be my honor."

"Ah, good. A'e you familia' with gung fu tea, Maste' Elliot?"

Elliot took a deep breath, paused, and then said, "Uh, yeah, well, I'm familiar. I've read a little about the gung fu tea ceremony on the Internet, but that's about it." Elliot was a little more than familiar with the gung fu ceremony. He had read everything he could find on the Internet about gung fu tea, which wasn't much. But he was able to get a rough idea of the ceremony. Elliot had also read several books on the subject of tea, including literature about Japanese tea and the Japanese tea ceremony *chanoyu*, or "hot water for tea." Elliot understood that chanoyu was very lengthy and had strict rules of etiquette, and participants drank *matcha*, a specific type of powdered green tea whipped to a froth with a small bamboo whisk.

Chanoyu did not appeal to Elliot. It seemed harsh and rigid, which intimidated him. Gung fu tea, on the other hand, seemed more relaxed to Elliot. Gung fu tea placed more emphasis on the tea and the social interaction between host and guest. There were fewer rules. One rule that Elliot knew about, which both ceremonies shared, was no talking about things that brought disharmony, such as politics, business, or other worldly things. Elliot knew that this included work and training—pretty much every aspect of his life—and this appealed to him very much. He spent his days thinking about these things, and he often dreamed of a place where he would be rescued from these thoughts and feelings, and that place was tea. "Good." The tea master turned and walked briskly toward the back room, where Elliot often saw him sitting. Elliot grabbed his things quickly and hurried after the old man, who was not waiting. They headed down the somewhat long hallway that Elliot had been down many times on his way to the restroom, which was the last door before the back room. The restroom door was so close to the back room where the shop owner spent most of his time that Elliot couldn't help but look into this room whenever he went to the restroom. And many times, he had made eye contact with the mysterious shop owner, who was always sitting on the floor at an uncharacteristically low table.

Every time Elliot glanced into the room, Chin Li would be staring, as if expecting Elliot to look in. The intense stare of the old man always startled Elliot and made him feel as if he were doing something wrong. Although Elliot would try to keep from looking into the room, his curiosity always got the best of him, and he found himself glancing in without realizing it until it was too late. The shock of the old man's stare, as if waiting for the young man to look in, hit Elliot like a punch to the head, leaving a sense of fear that lasted long after he left the teahouse. Now Elliot got to enter this room of intrigue—and he felt clumsy and uncertain.

Chin Li bowed at the door upon entering and then beckoned Elliot, who followed suit, also bowing before walking through the door. This was an etiquette Elliot practiced at his kung fu school. As Elliot walked past the tea master, he looked around. Though he had seen into the room many times, he had never more than glanced and had been too captive to Chin Li's stare to really see the room. So, finally getting to look around, he wondered at the near emptiness.

On the far left wall were two sets of shoji doors. Against the back wall were two single wooden chairs facing the center of the room and connected by a small table between them. Hanging on the front wall was a long scroll with beautifully painted Chinese characters. Elliot did not know what the characters meant but could not help but be mesmerized by the elegant beauty and grace of the large, hand-painted characters. Transfixed by the aesthetic design, Elliot forgot about Chin Li, who interrupted Elliot's gaze and said, "That sc'oll painted by good f'iend of mine. He was g'eat wa'io' and tea maste'. Sc'oll say, 'Th'ough blood of wa'io'.'"

Chin Li motioned Elliot toward the center of the room, where there were four large tatami mats that covered only a fraction of the dark wood floor. In the center of the tatami was a low rectangular table that was barely big enough for two people to sit at. The table was so low that the two men had to sit on the floor to use it. It was stained light brown in contrast to the dark wood floors and redwood borders that accented the room. The tabletop had small slits running in different directions, allowing water and tea to pass through into a hidden drip tray underneath. The tea master held out his hand toward one side of the table, indicating where Elliot should sit. Before sitting down himself, Chin Li walked back to the door and called out in Chinese to one of the servers working the salon, and then the old man sat across from Elliot.

Elliot tried to be casual about looking around the room, pretending Chin Li's gaze did not bother him. This went on for several long minutes as they sat in silence across from each other. Elliot tried desperately to think of casual things to ask the tea master but could only think of personal questions. *I wonder where he's from. He looks and sounds Chinese, and his name seems Chinese. But sometimes he says something or acts like maybe he's Japanese. Would it be rude to ask? That's probably bad etiquette. I wonder if he's a master. That* would *be bad etiquette to ask.*

"What a'e you thinking, young Maste' Elliot?"

"Oh, uh, nothing, really. I was just, uh, admiring the room. It's so...uh, relaxing, for lack of better word." He gave a quick but graceful look around.

"Ah, thank you, Maste' Elliot. 'The simplicity of the tea'oom and it f'eedom f'om vulga'ity make it t'uly a sanctua'y f'om the vexations of oute' world. The'e, and the'e alone, can one consec'ate himself to undistu'bed ado'ation of the beautiful.' Are you familia' with Kakuzo?"

Elliot wanted to say yes; he wanted Chin Li to know how smart he was and wished that he, too, could quote something beautiful. He was familiar with the author Chin Li referred to, having picked up his book on tea once at a bookstore. But, at the time, the book seemed difficult to understand, so he did not buy it. After reading other books on tea, Elliot had moved on to the subject of history and the sociology of warrior cultures, never going back for the book. "No. Well, I'm familiar with it but haven't read it yet."

Elliot, unable to hold eye contact, began looking around the empty room again while Chin Li held his gaze on Elliot. "That look is like you want ask me something but af'aid. Don't be af'aid. Only way fo' pe'son to t'uly lea'n is ask. If want to lea'n, Elliot, must ask."

Feeling extremely and suddenly intimidated by the old man's blunt assertion and penetrating stare, Elliot struggled with his response but finally said, "Uh, well, I...uh, in my kung fu training, I learn about etiquette, and, well, I don't want to breach etiquette by asking inappropriate questions. I...I don't want to offend you."

Chin Li pursed his lips slightly and gave a very subtle double nod in understanding and then said, "Fi'st best way lea'n is ask question; second best way, make mistake. He who make mistake neve' fo'get. You ask, make mistake, you double lea'n, Elliot."

Aware of another lesson from the tea master, Elliot thought for a while, and in a surprising moment of courage asked, "Uh, I was just wondering where you're from." He paused for a moment and then continued. "And, uh...well, I was kinda wondering if you've ever studied martial arts or just tea. You..." Elliot faltered slightly before concluding. "You seem, I mean, you make references to warriors and knowing warriors, and you've read *Hagakure*..." He finished with a slightly sheepish shrug that he tried to play off as jovial.

"Mmm," said Chin Li, shaking his head just a little. "No 'kinda.' Have confidence in question." His sudden slightly stern tone surprised Elliot again. It wasn't too harsh but sudden and different from the old man's usual demeanor.

Elliot fumbled out an apology. "Oh...uh, sorry." He feared for a moment that the tea master would correct his equally sudden apologetic behavior, and at that moment, Chin Li looked as though he were going to, but he simply gave a slight nod. Then Chin Li spoke, and his normal demeanor returned as suddenly as it had left, which surprised Elliot just as much. "I pa't Japanese, pa't Chinese. Ha-ha. I mix. My g'eat g'andfathe', he Japanese. He f'om long line of wa'io'. He move to China; teach Chinese how speak Japanese. That whe'e he meet Chinese wife. Have son. Du'ing Chinese people 'evolution g'eat g'and pa'ents flee China. Go Japan. They live with g'eat g'andfathe' family, where my g'andfathe' learn jujitsu, kendo, and chanoyu. But he not happy in Japan, so after g'ow up, he go China, lea'n diffe'ent ma'tial a't and gung fu tea. Become teache'. He only teache' teach women; that where he meet my g'andmothe'. They have son and daughte'. They son, my fathe'. Befo' Japan invade China in Wo'ld Wa' Two, they go Ame'ica. My fathe' teach me Japanese and Chinese cultu'e. Language, ma'tial a't, tea. When I old enough to t'avel, I go China, Taiwan, Japan to lea'n mo'e ma'tial a't and tea. In Japan, I study chanoyu f'om famous U'asenke maste'. He tell me sto'y about famous tea maste' defeat samu'ai. Afte' that, I focus on just tea. I t'avel and t'ain many yea', then come home open teahouse."

Elliot felt embarrassed. Not for Chin Li or because Chin Li had shared too much personal information. On the contrary, the information was exactly what Elliot had been curious about. Elliot's own fantasies about the mysterious shop owner being cultured, world traveled, and well trained were not far from what Chin Li had told him. Elliot was embarrassed because he had no interesting things to tell about himself. He had never traveled anywhere, was not trained in tea, and only been training in kung fu for a couple of years. He quickly thought of a question that would move the subject of conversation away from personal histories. "I'm sorry, did you say a tea master defeated a samurai?"

The wise old man noticed the intentional change of subject and allowed it. "Ah, yes, g'eat sto'y." And with a sudden but controlled excitement that revealed an almost childlike quality, the tea master continued. "In 1616, shogun issue dec'ee, *Ki'isute Gomen*, which mean 'to cut and leave.' It gave samu'ai 'ight to cut down anyone who offend them in slightest. One day, Maste' Seichi, teache' of chanoyu, offend samu'ai. This samu'ai easy to offend. Samu'ai have bad tempe'. Instead of cutting Seichi down, he say, 'meet me tomo'ow sun'ise; we have duel.' Seichi student of tea, neve' swo'd. But he have to meet samu'ai; it is law.

"Seichi not know what to do, so he go to f'iend, abbot of Zen temple. Abbot lead Seichi to temple tea'oom, ask Seichi lead chanoyu. When finish, Zen master tell Seichi he cannot defeat samu'ai with swo'd. But he would die with hono' if he app'oach combat same way as chanoyu. Zen maste' say, 'Wield swo'd st'aightfo'wa'dly, as you hold ladle in chanoyu, and applying same p'ecision and cla'ity of mind with which you pou' boiling wate' onto tea. Step fo'wa'd with no thought of consequence. St'ike th'ough cente' line of you' enemy! You cannot fail!'"

After a short pause, Chin Li went on. "Seichi emb'ace Zen maste' counsel and cast off all fea'. Next mo'ning, Seichi stand at meeting spot on top of hill outside village. He stand in deep meditation. As samu'ai app'oach, he stop, stunned and f'ozen at se'enity and 'adiant p'esence he had not expected. Samu'ai say, 'Excuse me, so so'y!' And the samu'ai bow deeply and walk away."

In the abrupt silence that followed the conclusion of the story, Elliot processed the unbelievable events and the morals in the story. He recognized obvious kung fu lessons and could not help but identify with them. He almost immediately thought of a quote from Sun Tzu: *"The supreme art of war is to subdue the enemy without ever going to battle."* Elliot had read Sun Tzu before he had started training in kung fu, and he had been required to read it again by his sifu. It was often the topic of conversation in kung fu class.

During the long silence after the story, Chin Li just stared at Elliot searchingly with a look that broke Elliot's concentration and made it hard for him to return the gaze. "So, Maste' Elliot, tell me whe'e f'om?"

Elliot tried to think of something—some way to embellish his life—to impress the tea master, but the question warranted an immediate reply, and under Chin Li's unwavering look, Elliot confessed, "Well, there's not much to tell really. I grew up not far from here, and after school, I went to work." And Elliot gave a subtle frown and a slight shrug.

"What you pa'ents do fo' living?"

Elliot was never sure how to answer this question. He was never comfortable talking about his parents because he was as embarrassed about them. He was embarrassed that they were never around, and it had been well known in school that Elliot was poor and a bastard; popular topics for the other students to ridicule him about.

Elliot felt more despondent because he did not want to go into his personal life, especially his parents. But he felt trapped, and once again under the weight of Chin Li's stare, he broke. "Uh, well, my dad was never around growing up. He left my mom before I was born. And my mom, she always worked factory jobs during the day and a lot of times worked as a waitress in the evenings." Elliot unintentionally thought back to growing up and being alone all the time. As he lost himself momentarily in his past, he tried, as he always did, to picture his mother's face but could not.

Realizing it was too uncomfortable a topic, Chin Li decided to change the subject a little bit. "Did you go college, Elliot?"

Elliot let out a slow, unintentional sigh and furrowed his brows slightly as he came out of his trance and turned his thoughts to college, another painful chapter in his life. "No... no, I went straight into the workforce." He felt shame, as he always did when he thought about college. He'd had such a hard time in high school socially that he could not bear the thought of college.

Chin Li could again sense uneasiness in Elliot and simply said, "College not fo' eve'yone. Beside, life bette' teache'."

Then Elliot, to his own surprise and before he could stop himself, did something he was not accustomed to. He opened up a little bit and confessed some of his true feelings, including a secret he had never told anyone. "I couldn't get into a good college anyway, even if I had wanted to. Not to mention, I wouldn't have been able to afford it. I wasn't going to qualify for any scholarships, that's for sure."

Elliot paused and let out a sarcastic laugh before continuing, "For a long time, I was a nerd in school. Good grades, all that stuff...but I wanted people to like me. People didn't like nerds." He let out another sarcastic laugh. "I decided that if I wanted people to like me, I needed to stop being a nerd. So I started getting bad grades. I stopped turning in assignments, I did poorly on tests on purpose, and when I was called on to answer a question, I'd give some witty incorrect answer to make everyone laugh.

"Hmm, it didn't work though. It never made anyone laugh. In fact, it just gave everyone more things to make fun of me for. My grade-point average went from 3.99 to almost failing. Which, of course, people made fun of me for." Elliot let out yet another laugh. "It's almost funny now, the irony. Everyone made fun of me for doing well in school, getting good grades, following the rules...then I did the opposite: I got bad grades, didn't follow rules..."

Realizing he had digressed a little from his point, he went on. "I just barely graduated, and it did nothing but ensure that I wouldn't get into a good college. Everyone still hated me and treated me like shit." Elliot didn't even notice that he had cursed in front of the respectable old man.

When he snapped out of his trance-like state, Chin Li was still staring at him, but it was a different look. It was a familiar look that Elliot had noticed on his sifu on occasion. He had always found the look peculiar—distinct. He was never sure what the look meant or what his sifu was thinking, but it was a particular look, a defined look, and now Chin Li had it.

After several moments, Chin Li changed the topic again. It's not that he didn't care about Elliot's feelings or that he didn't want to hear Elliot's story. On the contrary, Chin Li was very interested. However, his job as host was to make the guests of a tea ceremony feel happy and at peace, to invoke serenity and a sense of being at one with nature. Strict rules of tea etiquette dictated that no conversation should involve anything that would cause distress to the guest or upset the harmony of the ceremony. The old man asked, "What get you inte'ested in tea?"Elliot did not want to admit that he had read somewhere that tea may help with depression. He felt he had already revealed too much about himself. But he was glad Chin Li had changed the subject. As casually as he could, Elliot replied, "Actually, I read somewhere that tea was really good for you, so I thought I'd give it a try. Plus, the job I was working at the time was a factory job where I sat down all day, which made me drowsy. Since I hate coffee, I thought tea was the answer. I researched tea online to learn more about it and tried to find good tea. I never thought to check the phone book or Internet for tea salons in the area. I came across this place by accident one day while out walking. After that, I looked for other tea salons or shops in the area, but the few I found were more English style."

Elliot sat for a while, sinking back into a trance, though not a bad one. He thought back to when he first started drinking tea. "After I finally found good tea...ahhh, I remember how it made me feel. The best was at work. The job I had at the time...I was allowed to have food and drink at my workstation, and every time I took a drink, for a brief moment...for that brief moment...I was transported out of there and taken away to some lazy summer afternoon with warm sun, cool breezes...freedom. I was taken away to freedom, and it was so real, so lifelike, like I was really there." Elliot awoke from his trance to find Chin Li smiling broadly at him. Elliot was again suddenly embarrassed at yet another uncontrolled expression of his feelings. Elliot feared that these revelations would lead the tea master to determine that Elliot was not the warrior the old man thought he was.

"That is good, Elliot. That is the flowe'."

This statement caused another uncontrolled reaction from Elliot: a smile. Elliot found himself trying to hold the smile in. But the harder he tried, the bigger his smile grew. He recognized the flower reference from an old Buddhist parable about a Buddhist disciple understanding Chan when his master picks up a flower and looks at it. But Elliot's smile faded as he reminded himself that he didn't understand Chan, nor had he ever understood the parable that he had heard his sifu tell many times. Chin Li, seeing Elliot's smile fade away, said, "That is way of Chan: the'e fo' moment, then gone, change something else. Always change."

The tea master got up and walked over to the white sliding doors and opened one of them. Behind the door was a shelf full of books. Elliot could see that a lot of the books were in English, and a lot had Chinese characters on them. The old man reached in and pulled one out. While looking at the cover and with his back still to Elliot, Chin Li quoted from the book, "The whole ideal of teaism is a 'esult of the Chan conception of g'eatness in the smallest incidents of life." Then Chin Li turned, walked over to Elliot, and with both hands and a slight bow, handed the book to Elliot. It was a copy of *The Book of Tea* by Okakura Kakuzo. Elliot didn't know what to say. It was not common for someone to give him a gift. He stared at the book, feeling that he should not accept it. He struggled with what to say. Elliot was unsure how to even accept a gift, let alone how not to accept one. But he so desperately wanted to accept it that, in his gripping stupor, he uttered, "Uh...wow...thanks," while Chin Li sat back down.

"You a'e welcome, Elliot. It is must 'ead fo' any adept student of tea. You must 'ead then tell me what you think."

Just as Chin Li finished, two servers came into the room with trays. They both knelt down beside the host and guest and carefully placed a pot, cups, aroma cups, a pitcher, and what looked like a tiny vase with tea utensils in it on the table. Elliot had seen the equipage on the Internet and knew that everything was small but was shocked at how miniscule everything actually was. It all seemed as tiny as a child's play set. The teapot itself held so little that Elliot knew he could drink the contents in one easy gulp. One of the servers set a large cast-iron kettle and trivet on one side of the table. Everything was very plain and simple yet held an aura of extravagance. The kettle—with its rustic lower half scorched from years of use, simple hailstone upper half, and lid lined with a subtle hint of rust—was nothing out of the ordinary, yet it demanded attention to its aesthetic beauty.

The teapot seemed a guest of honor in the entourage of equipage, although it sat humbly, being even plainer than the kettle with its smooth contoured surface, its figure flowing in elegant curves. And though the pot and kettle differed in size, color, shape, and function, they did not argue. They sat together in harmony, embodying the true essence of tea, where everyone is the same—equal no matter their status. All other members of the tea set followed suit, with their presence of plainness and modesty while maintaining their own identities.

The whole ensemble was so simple in its beauty and more beautiful in its simplicity. But the art was neither in the individual pieces, nor in the *kakemono* hanging on the wall, nor in the subtle artistic design in the room's architecture. Nor did these things dictate the tea experience. It was a true master who created the experience. It was he who made the art come alive. Through the skill of the tea master, the guest did not just enjoy the taste of tea and the art of the ceremony but became the art itself—was transformed, becoming a unique work of art different from any other before and any other to come, captured in a single moment. The tea master would hypnotize his guests by hearkening to the senses. The beautiful array of soft, subtle colors would capture the eyes; incense gently wafting through the air would tease and lure the nose; perhaps nature music or the sounds of a river playing quietly in the background or just the kettle would sing softly in the ears; and the taste of the sweet elixir, so seductive, like the yin essence of a woman satisfying and not satisfying at the same time, would leave the guests always wanting more. It was truly tea that launched a thousand ships, inciting wars and revolutions and forging nations.

Elliot watched the steam rise and dance to the drama that was being played out as Chin Li poured first hot water and then hot tea over everything before preparing tea to drink. The tea master bowed slightly as he offered Elliot the first cup, and Elliot returned the bow as he took the cup with both hands. As Elliot rested his right hand in his lap and held the tiny drink in his left, waiting for an indication of when he should drink, the tea master said, "No, no, Elliot. Must hold in 'ight hand; 'ight hand swo'd hand. Tea embody peace and ha'mony; must put down swo'd and emb'ace peace and ha'mony."

It was not a harsh correction, only a simple instruction on etiquette, and had no impact on the serenity of the moment. For a split second, Elliot felt embarrassment flicker in him, but it quickly passed as he switched hands and was motioned by the host to drink. As Elliot raised the cup to his lips, which was not even half a mouthful, the tea master once again intervened, "Must d'ink in at least th'ee d'inks o' mo'e. Main fundamental of tea is mode'ation."

Elliot held his cup up and gave a slight bow of gratitude to his host, who returned the gesture, and they both drank. And so Chin Li prepared and served Elliot tea, and the two sat in a comfortable silence. Elliot's thoughts were not happy, sad, distraught, awkward, uncomfortable, or embarrassed; for once, he just *was*. He did not stop to contemplate his sense of harmony.

Several cups of tea later, Elliot suddenly awoke from what seemed like a dream. His eyes had been open the whole time, but he had been lost in an unconscious serenity, and when he woke, Chin Li was, as usual, staring intently at him. "You know, Elliot, the'e is old Chinese custom: if host offe' second cup of tea, he good host. If he offe' thi'd cup of tea, it mean guest has ove'stayed welcome. Ha-ha. Beside, Lu Yu say, 'One should not d'ink mo'e than th'ee cups of tea unless ext'emely thi'sty.' Ha-ha." The distinct chuckle warmed Elliot even more.

Though Chin Li spoke in jest, Elliot got the message loud and clear. "Well, it's getting late. I don't know how to thank you for the...uh...," and he gestured toward the entire tea equipage for the ceremony. "It's really probably the best... uh, I guess I don't know how to say thank you."

"Simple, Elliot. Just say 'thank you.'" Taking note of Elliot's struggle to say thank you, the wise old tea master said, "You must not say 'thank you' ve'y much."

"Uh, well, nobody's ever...nobody ever, uh...," and suddenly realizing he was about to reveal more personal information, Elliot quickly said, "I mean, thank you very much. It's the nicest thing anyone has ever done for me."

Chin Li understood what Elliot almost said and replied, "Ha-ha, you must know lot of je'ks, Elliot." And once again, the genuine humor of the tea master rescued Elliot from his thoughts. "Befo'e you go, I have gift fo' you." Then Chin Li got up.

"Oh no, you've done enough already. I mean the tea, the tea book...I already don't know how to repay you." Elliot got up to intercept the old man as he spoke.

"You no have to 'epay, Elliot. These gifts, not ba'te'. Besides, no a'gue, Elliot—bad etiquette, ve'y bad." Despite the seriousness of this statement, the old man chuckled again as he walked back over to the white sliding doors.

The statement, attitude, and action of Chin Li had such finality that Elliot didn't know what to say or do. He stood frozen, suddenly uncomfortable again. He felt fear envelop him as he grasped the situation, knowing he was going to have to accept or deny another gift. Elliot was momentarily distracted by the indecision of which was harder.

Chin Li opened one of the sliding doors, which revealed boxes and miscellaneous tea wares. The old man took out a large, obviously used paper bag and began putting small boxes and other things in it. Holding the bag in one hand and a tiny box in the other, the tea master finally turned to Elliot. Chin Li sat the bag down and opened the box to reveal a tiny teapot much like the one he had just used to serve Elliot tea. "Gung fu teapots ve'y special. Made f'om special clay. They call *yixing* pots. Afte' yea's of use, they abso'b flavo' of tea. Must only use one kind of tea. Ve'y important, Elliot. Use diffe'ent teas, make pot taste bad, make tea taste bad. Look, a good teapot sings." And the old man took the lid and dragged it around the rim of the little pot. The noise from this action echoed that of a wet finger being run over the rim of a crystal wine glass. And like a crystal glass, the pot sang. But it did not sing of extravagance and high living. It sang of quiet retreats, slow rivers, and beauty in simplicity. "This pot al'eady seasoned. I put tea in bag. When you 'un out, come and see me; I give you mo'e. Use only this tea. Ve'y impo'tant. Tea not on menu; I give f'om pe'sonal stash."

Chin Li put the pot back into the small, plain box and put it in the bag. "This all you need fo' gung fu tea. 'Emembe', skill come f'om effo't. Must p'actice. Tea is simple. In the wo'd of g'eat Tea Maste' Rikyu, 'Tea is nothing othe' than heating wate', p'epa'ing tea, and d'inking with p'op'iety. That all you need to know.'"

Elliot stood there, even more shocked than before. While he had wrestled with whether he should or shouldn't accept another gift, he hadn't considered what the gift would be, and he would have never thought it would be something so great. How could he accept such a gift? How could he say thanks to all this? The words did not do his gratitude justice. "Chin Li, this is too much. I don't know..."

"Just say 'thank you,' Elliot. That all you need." And Chin Li stood calmly and patiently, with an air of humbleness, satisfaction, and sternness as he waited for Elliot's thank-you.

Elliot could once again sense finality in Chin Li and knew that the old man was not going to take no for an answer. As the moment grew long, the tea master's look and demeanor—his very aura—changed. It wasn't hostile. Elliot wasn't sure what it was, but it felt heavy. Even the air suddenly felt thick. It was as if his very senses were being attacked. He had never experienced such a feeling, and it suddenly invoked a fear in him that he'd never felt before.

Finally, under the weight of the unseen power emitting from the tea master, Elliot uttered, "Uh, thank you. Thank you very much. I don't...I don't know what to say. If there's... anything I can do for you, ever, anything I could do for you, please...just ask." Elliot searched desperately for something more to say or offer or do, but to no avail.

Suddenly, the weight in the room lifted, and the old master's demeanor changed back like the sudden passing of a storm. "You a'e ve'y welcome, Elliot. But the'e is something you can do fo' me."

Excited at the prospect of repaying the generous tea master, Elliot quickly blurted out, "Anything!"

"Continue lea'ning a't of tea, its cultu'e and histo'y, and sha'e it. And numbe' two, come back tomo'ow. I have anothe' gift fo' you."

Elliot began to protest. He felt even more shame at the idea of receiving another gift from Chin Li. But Chin Li interrupted Elliot's protest. Holding up his hand and shaking his head, Chin Li said, "You ask what you can do fo' me. You can show me p'ope' etiquette and not a'gue." And in the flash of a moment, the stern demeanor came and went before Chin Li continued. "Come by tomo'ow, and I give you one mo'e gift."

Elliot was embarrassed by Chin Li's rebuke, and he gave a bow and apologized. He did not dare refuse.

After leaving the teahouse, Elliot rushed home and immediately got out the tea set with which the old man had gifted him. It was already late, and he was afraid to drink any more tea out of fear that it would keep him awake, so he set everything up and inspected the individual pieces over and over, feeling euphoric at receiving the nicest gifts he'd ever gotten. His mother was the only person who had ever given him anything, and though he'd appreciated everything she'd ever gotten him, the gifts were always necessities—clothing or school supplies. But Elliot knew that his mother had worked hard and hadn't made enough money to go beyond necessity.

Elliot was too excited to spend much time thinking about his mother. He continued inspecting the tea ware and going through the motions of the gung fu tea ceremony. However, even in his ecstasy, he could feel work tugging, pulling, and jerking at his conscience as the night grew later. And this relentless pull deteriorated his mood into melancholy. He wished he had the nerve to call in sick so he could stay home and practice gung fu tea. But the thought of calling in made him nauseous at the possibility of any kind of confrontation, whether being questioned during the phone call or the next day when he returned to work. In his whole life, including throughout school, he had only missed a few days, and though he had been truly ill, each time he had been questioned on the phone or harassed the next day by bosses. So he gave up the mere thought of calling in and went to bed, dozing off while reading and falling in love with Kakuzo.

four

There are only two forces in the world, the sword and the spirit. In the long run, the sword will always be conquered by the spirit.
—Napoleon Bonaparte

At work, Elliot could not stop thinking about the previous night. Replaying the whole evening over and over again in his head, he tried to relive every detail. He thought a lot about Chin Li and the old man's generosity—everything he had done and the gifts—and wondered what other gift the tea master could possibly give him next. Every once in a while, he would hear a voice in his head that would question the old tea-shop owner's sincerity, a voice that always called into question people's motives and intentions. And Chin Li was exceptionally kind and interested. *Why? Why would a respected tea master and business owner care about me? Of all the people that come into his salon...NO! I'm not going to ruin it. If he didn't really like me, he wouldn't give me gifts. I don't care why he likes me; he just does.* And Elliot quickly dismissed his doubt and thought more about Chin Li's kindness and the gung fu tea ceremony.

Although work was as long and relentless as usual, Elliot was quick to forget about work when it was time to leave. After rushing home and cleaning up, he quickly went to the teahouse, almost unable to contain his excitement. This magnitude of excitement was unfamiliar to Elliot, and he struggled to control it. When he got to WabiCha, he went in and, as calmly as he could, asked to see the owner.

"So'y, Chin Li ve'y busy 'ight now. He say please wait, have tea, and he be with you soon."

Elliot's only disappointment was that he didn't bring a book or something, as he had not anticipated having to wait. He had been there before without something to read or do and had felt very awkward just sitting there, trying not to look at people. "Uh, yeah, yeah, thank you."

"OK, what you want? Usual? Lung Ching—Dragon Well."

"Uh, yes, please. Thank you." Elliot had long known the translation of *lung ching* and momentarily felt a little pride at his knowledge of tea. He sat down at a vacant table. It did not take the server long to return with his tea, and he took his time preparing it, knowing that once he was done he'd have nothing to do but stare around the tiny salon. The table he was sitting at was far from the small front windows, and the salon was crowded. There were people everywhere he glanced. After a few long moments of trying to not look awkward or directly at people, two beautiful girls sat down to his right. Right away, he felt more uncomfortable. He had a very difficult time not looking over at them because they were sitting so near. Not having a lot of experience with women, he was very intimidated by them, especially pretty ones.

The girl sitting directly beside him had long blond hair with highlights and suspiciously blue eyes. The girl across from her and catty-corner to Elliot was more in his line of sight, and she had medium-length, light-brown, straight hair; medium skin tone; and light-blue—almost green—eyes. Although her facial features were nothing like Briseis's, the girl reminded him of her. Briseis was Elliot's one very short-lived romance and thus had become his standard for women. The brown-haired girl and Elliot shared a couple of glances, and the girl smiled slightly and receptively. Elliot uncontrollably returned her smile with his own sheepish and awkward smile.

Finally the brown-haired girl asked with an air of humor and a very youthful giggle, "Excuse me, I don't mean to pry, but I...we couldn't help noticing you are sitting alone, and knowing how bad that sucks, we were wondering, are you alone on purpose or is someone standing you up?"

Elliot was immediately shocked. Although he was typically suspicious of girls and their intentions, he sensed she was being friendly. But despite his utter surprise and with his guard up, he quickly and casually responded with an equal bit of humor. "Uh, no, I'm actually that guy who likes to come to small, crowded places alone and pretend like he's not uncomfortable." When he heard himself speak, he was shocked at the casualness of his reply. The thought of speaking to girls usually frightened him to the point that it rendered him speechless. The only girl he had ever really spoken to this casually was Briseis, and, for a brief moment, Briseis ran through his mind, and he felt warm and happy.

Both girls giggled and looked at each other. Then the brown-haired girl asked again, "No, really, are you alone?"

"Actually, I'm friends with Chin Li, the owner, and I was supposed to meet him today, but he's busy at the moment. I didn't anticipate him being busy, and I didn't bring anything to read, so..." He gave a slight shrug. "My name is Elliot, by the way." He reached over and offered the girl his hand.

"Oh, I'm Chrissie, and this is—"

"I'm Linzy."

He shook both of their hands in turn and said, "Pleasure to meet you."

Elliot was very careful of the things he said and kept the conversation light. He did not want to be sucked into a conversation about his job. They were both students, and when Chrissie asked him what he did, he told them he was a student of martial arts and its history and philosophies. He went on to say that he was an assistant instructor in training. This seemed to impress the girls, and they weren't a bit disturbed when he reluctantly told them what his day job was, being careful to use the term "manufacturing" instead of "factory worker" and leaving out the gory details.

As the conversation went on, the girls asked about his training, and he asked about their schooling and humored them whenever he could. The conversation flowed, and Elliot felt uncharacteristically comfortable. But inevitably and suddenly, the conversation died. Before it got awkward, Linzy said, "Well, Chrissie, I have to get back," and she gave her friend an odd look. "I'm going to go pay. I'll be right back." She gave Chrissie another odd glance that Elliot couldn't read.

Elliot wasn't sure what was going on or what the looks were about. The whole meeting and conversation had happened so fast, and the conclusion was happening faster. Elliot felt panic. The moment was over. But then something strange happened. He spoke, as if someone else were speaking for him. "So you want to get together sometime and maybe have dinner or something?" It was casual and inconsequential, as if it didn't matter if she did or not. But it did. He was paralyzed—frozen in a long moment, as if the quickness of their meeting had to stop and let time catch up.

"Yeah, sure. Let me give you my number."

Suddenly, the girls were gone. When Elliot snapped out of his stupor at what had just transpired, he found himself in a peculiar mood. He wasn't ecstatic like he thought he should be, or even excited. The way he felt wasn't exactly bland, either, and it was more than satisfied. He was just...happy.

Elliot sat for a long time after Chrissie and Linzy had left, but he no longer felt awkward. He didn't even notice all the people around him, nor did he realize he was just staring into space. Feeling fully content, he had forgotten that he was waiting on Chin Li and was again startled by the old shop owner. "Ah, young Maste' Elliot, so so'y keep you waiting," and he gave a slight bow.

Elliot got up and said, "Oh, no, it's OK. I was just, uh... enjoying some tea." And he returned the bow.

"Ah, you must have fallen in love while you wait on me. You look smitten, Maste' Elliot." Chin Li gave that old-kung fu-movie laugh as he turned toward the back of the salon. Elliot began following Chin Li and wondered if the shop owner had been watching him or if it was the tea master's exceptional intuition. Elliot was constantly overwhelmed with disbelief at his new friend's ability to perceive so much by merely look-ing at someone.

When they got to the tearoom in the back of the salon, Chin Li walked to the host's side of the low table and knelt down, looking at an old, long, thin case that lay across the tea table. Elliot knelt down opposite the tea master, where he had sat the night before. "You know, Maste' Elliot, I know you' sifu. He ve'y good teache'. Good pe'son. He a g'eat wa'io'."

Elliot was shocked at this revelation. Elliot had mentioned his sifu to the tea master before, but the old man had said nothing of their acquaintance. Chin Li paused for a long moment, still staring at the long case, and then continued. "I believe eve'y wa'io' should know way of the swo'd. Swo'd extension of body. You' sifu good teache', but he not teach way of the swo'd." Chin Li opened the case, and in it was a katana, a samurai sword. Maintaining his intense stare on the katana, the old tea master went on. "In ancient Japan, they say swo'd have soul of its own, and wa'io' and swo'd become one—kind'ed spi'its. The swo'd become soul of wa'io'."

Chin Li picked up the sheathed weapon and slowly inspected it. "It also believed that swo'd smith pe'sonality embodied in eve'y blade and that if his soul was bad, the swo'd would be bad, and the wa'io' wielding swo'd become bad. One of Japan's most famous swo'd smiths, Senzo Mu'amasa, made some of Japan's most famous swo'd, but he was a violent man, and the wielde's of his swo'ds all become kille's or kill themselves. But some of Mu'amasa student make excellent swo'd, and they not mad, so thei' swo'd not evil. My ances-tor was one of Mu'amasa student. He make many swo'd fo' my Japanese side of family. It believed that swo'd choose its owne'. This one neve' found owne'." Then the tea master held the sword up with two hands and bowed as he handed it to Elliot.

In utter disbelief, Elliot froze for a long time, at first not realizing that the sword was the gift, and then shook his head. "Oh, no, I couldn't...it's too much. This is way too much."

But the old tea master simply said, "Maste' Elliot, this ve'y special gift. It ve'y dis'espectful fo' you not accept. You not accept, we cannot be f'iends." The old man lowered his gaze back down to a bow while still holding the sword out to Elliot. Elliot bowed low before taking the katana. Mesmerized, he looked the sword over very slowly. "I've...never owned a sword before. Uh, honestly, I... I know nothing about them." And he just sat in quiet disbelief at the unbelievable gift. Even more unbelievable to Elliot was not the priceless gift that Chin Li was bestowing upon him but the overwhelming sense of friendship. *Why? Of all of the people...of everyone who comes into the salon...out of everyone...why me? Why do I deserve his friendship...and all of these gifts? Who am I?*

"Ah, fi'st 'ule of etiquette is, when showing someone you' weapon, neve' fully d'aw it f'om sheath. Second 'ule: neve' touch pe'son's weapon without pe'mission. That 'ule fo' all weapon. Ve'y impo'tant. So, if I may?" And again the tea master bowed as he held his hands out to receive back the katana.

Elliot, still in shock, bowed again as he returned the weapon with both hands. "That good, Elliot. That thi'd 'ule: always bow when give o' 'eceive weapon. Now, when you want to inspect o' show someone blade, you pull pa'tway out." Chin Li pulled the blade partway out of its sheath, exposing several inches of polished steel.

Elliot could not only see the sharpness of the blade but also sense it. And though Elliot was not aware of the significance of the *hamon*, the tempering pattern, or the *hada*, the grain of the forged steel, the beauty slashed out at him, sharper than the edge itself. He was so mesmerized by the beauty of the blade that he didn't notice the plainness of the brass *habaki* or the simple lotus *tsuba*. He wasn't sure if it was Chin Li's influence or what the old man had said about swords having their own souls, but Elliot was sure he sensed something, like another presence in the room. He dismissed this notion and attributed it overactive imagination.

Chin Li shut the blade back into the sheath and once again bowed as he handed the weapon to Elliot, who received it appropriately. Now noticing the simply designed hand guard and the expertly wrapped hilt, he could feel the countless hands that had gripped the sword over its life span. Elliot exposed the appropriate amount of steel and again stared, transfixed, at his gift as the overall beauty hypnotized him. All emotion had left him, and time didn't stop for him like it normally did—it ceased existing altogether, and he was left in overwhelming awe.

"Now I teach you *iaido*, the a't of d'awing swo'd. Simply d'awing swo'd is attack. When in combat, when have to d'aw swo'd, make it attack, always attack." And once again, the old man was bowing and holding out his hands to receive the sword.

It took Elliot several moments to wake from his euphoria and register that Chin Li was waiting. Elliot looked up at his friend and returned the weapon. "D'aw and cut ve'y impo'tant—*ichigeki hissatsu*. One motion. D'aw and cut—not two motion, one!" The old man stood up and, for a long time, remained unmoving like a statue, and Elliot felt as if the old tea-shop owner suddenly looked different...younger. He saw that distinct look on the tea master's face that he had seen the night before. Then, like a sudden explosion, Chin Li shouted, "Kiai!" and in one motion, faster than Elliot could see, the old man stomped one foot forward, drew the mystic blade, and slashed through the air. Elliot's entire body was imprisoned by the shock, leaving him in utter confusion, as if all life was suddenly gone and all that was left was a warrior standing before him. Then the young warrior turned back into an old tea master. Chin Li looked down at Elliot, and all life returned.

In one, quick, smooth motion, Chin Li sheathed the weapon, held it up, and looked intently at it for several moments before looking back at Elliot. When the tea master broke his stare from the weapon, Elliot saw the distinct and mysterious look vanish, and the old tea master said, "Kiai' ve'y impo'tant. It where all powe' come f'om. Now you t'y. Fi'st, d'aw and cut, one motion. Then sheath you' weapon, and t'y again. Late' I show you d'aw, cut, and sheath one motion, but fi'st must maste' d'aw and cut. Then sheath weapon. Always sheath weapon. Ve'y impo'tant."

Elliot took the weapon and did exactly as he had seen the old man do and exactly as the old man instructed. Slow and steady, Elliot drew the sword for the tea master, who gave him pointers and reminded him to shout "kiai." He did not feel silly or stupid or embarrassed, the feelings he often felt at kung fu. It was never his sifu who made Elliot feel this way, it was Elliot himself. But somehow Chin Li had a way of making Elliot feel comfortable and confident. Although he still felt a little awkward and clumsy, he noticed a subtle familiarity with the way the sword handled, a natural feeling.

"Ah, I suspected," the tea master said after a few of Elliot's attempts. "They say a swo'd chooses its owne', not owne' choose swo'd. This swo'd been a'ound long time, many gene'ation, but neve' pick owne'. Something about you tell me you pe'fect match fo' this stubbo'n blade. Ha-ha, I knew the'e something about you, young Maste' Elliot." The tea master continued to chuckle.

Elliot stopped his training and stared at the sword. "Master Chin, I know you say I should take this gift...and I want to, I really do, but this is an heirloom...a priceless heirloom. I mean, it's antique and authentic...outside the sentimental value..."

With his distinct chuckle, the old man cut in. "Ah, Maste' Elliot, as I say befo'e, the'e a'e many swo'ds like this in my family. All membe' of my family have swo'd. This swo'd not choose any of them. Include me. Ha-ha, ha-ha. This swo'd in possession of many membe's of my family and fail to find wo'thy owne'. They pass to me, say, 'Li, find wo'thy owne'.' We not ca'e about money, Elliot. It mo'e impo'tant to us that it belong to someone who will use it fo' good—hono' it. Not hang on wall to show off to 'ich f'iends. Take this gift, Maste' Elliot. Use it, become 'ighteous, and pass on t'adition of swo'd, t'adition of Bushido, way of wa'io'."

* * *

Although Elliot rushed home, it was already late into the evening. Barely containing his excitement, he moved his coffee table and some other furniture in his tiny living room so he had room for iaido. Unlike his experience at WabiCha, Elliot felt very silly about shouting "kiai" and barely uttered the powerful word at first. And each time he did, he felt more and more stupid until he stopped completely. Over and over, he drew and slashed at the air, but something didn't feel right. He knew he wasn't going to master it in one evening, but he had felt something at the tea salon that he was not feeling any more: confidence.

Elliot sat down, trying desperately to hold fast to the feeling of euphoria and confidence that had coursed through him earlier. *Damn it!* He was not losing his sense of euphoria to sadness, as he expected, but to frustration. He hit the edge of the sofa with his fist, got up, and began drawing and cutting again. Again and again, he drew and cut. His frustration boiled over to anger, and he started to sense something—feel something—but it still wasn't what he had felt at the teahouse. It was another sensation with which he was not too familiar. It was very similar to what he had felt during his last conversation with his sifu. Finally, and to his own surprise, "kiai" burst forth from deep within him, and in that moment, he felt as if he transcended time and space.

His sword didn't slash through space; it became space, and then it ceased. He tried again and again, shouting "kiai!" And though he did not achieve the effect he had just had in that one moment, he did feel something.

Pound, pound, pound...

"Hey, Elliot! Shut the fuck up over there!"

Elliot was not surprised or offended at his neighbor Drew's behavior—it was not uncommon for his neighbor to be rude or disrespectful—and it was getting late. He barely registered what his neighbor even said. He just stopped and held the mighty blade and stared at it for a long while. After getting into bed, Elliot held the sheathed sword in his hands, unable to sleep, but it was not the usual depressed insomnia—it was warm happiness that kept him awake well into the night.

The next morning, Elliot did something he had done only a couple of times in his whole life: he called into work, except this time he felt no fear or guilt. He spent the day practicing the sword and gung fu tea, and with all his neighbors, especially his rude neighbor Drew, at work, he could shout "kiai" as loud and as much as he wanted. He also spent a good part of the day thinking about Chin Li and all of the kindness and wisdom the old man had showered upon him. Elliot thought again about the way the old tea master was always quoting some classic book or person, and it inspired him to memorize lines and passages from his favorite books. In between tea and *kendo,* the way of the sword, Elliot browsed through one of his many favorite books, looking for great lines or wisdom he could memorize and quote. And all day long, he studied, drank tea, and drew his magnificent blade. But for once in his life, in a cruel twist of irony, time sped up as if to rob Elliot of his day of bliss. Elliot didn't mind much, though. He was actually looking forward to going to kung fu class to tell his sifu all that had transpired.

There was something else that Elliot could hardly wait for. He was waiting until the evening to call Chrissie. Elliot was so ecstatic about the precious gifts and lessons Chin Li had bestowed upon him that he had hardly thought about his new acquaintance. He was also afraid to think about Chrissie too much because he knew he would end up discouraging himself. He tried very hard not to get too excited because he didn't want to end up saying or doing anything that would jeopardize the potential of an ongoing relationship with the beautiful young girl.

Another reason he tried so hard not to think about Chrissie, a reason he didn't want to admit to himself, was that every time he thought about her, he could not help but think about Briseis and wonder where she was, what she was doing, or who she was with. Every time Briseis popped into his head, he quickly thought of something else because no matter how happy he was, the slightest thought of her sent a wave of sadness through him. Of all the moments in Elliot's life where he blew a chance or opportunity at something great because of his fear and insecurities, Briseis was the one that haunted him most. *But Chrissie is beautiful...just as beautiful,* he told himself, but deep down, he knew it wasn't true; no one was as beautiful as Briseis. He was nonetheless very excited about meeting a girl, getting to know her, and being with her. With the exception of that one moment eons ago, he had not known a woman.

When Elliot got to the *kwoon*, the kung fu school, he immediately went to his sifu's office, where he found his teacher and kung fu brother Sihing Horvath talking. "Elliot, how are you?" Sifu Miller bowed before Elliot had a chance to.

As Elliot bowed, he replied with an almost childlike excitement, "Good, Sifu, how are you?" and then he bowed to his sihing in turn, who was already bowing.

Sifu seemed to sense the unusual excitement coming from Elliot, who continued, "Sifu, I have had the best luck the past couple of days."

"Really? Good! Tell us what's happened."

With excitement bursting forth, Elliot began his tale. "Well, the other day I was at this place, WabiCha Teahouse, and the owner, Chin Li, came out and started talking to me."

"Ah, you met Master Chin," interrupted Sifu, who gave a slight grin. Austin, who was sitting in one of the chairs opposite Sifu Miller and looking at the ground, revealed a slight smile.

"He mentioned he knew you," Elliot said, indicating Sifu.

"Yeah, I—we know him," replied Sifu, and Austin allowed more of a chuckle to escape this time as he subtly shook his head up and down in an affirming way. "Did he serve you tea?"

Elliot's excitement began to abate. "Yeah, yeah, he did..." Then Elliot paused for a moment and wondered, suspicious that they had been served tea by the eccentric tea master as well. *Is this something he did for everyone? Does he just serve anyone tea?* And for a brief moment, the tea ceremony he had shared with the old shop owner felt less special. But he quickly dismissed his suspicion and jealousy. "And afterward, he gave me stuff to serve tea, like in gung fu tea ceremony."

"Wow, really?" The other two seemed a bit surprised at this revelation.

"That's not all. He told me to come back the next day, which was yesterday, and he had something else for me. It was a sword, a katana—a samurai sword. And not just any sword—his ancestor was a famous sword maker in Japan, and he made it!" Elliot could barely control his excitement.

Now the two men were really surprised, and Sifu Miller said, "Wow, he must have taken a real liking to you." And he and Austin sat there, smiles replaced by looks of shock and approval.

Elliot almost cut his sifu off when he said, "He even showed me some stuff—some techniques with the sword."

Sifu Miller was so surprised that he almost didn't know what to say. "Well...wow, that's really...great. Chin Li's a very kind man, among many other things. He's done a lot for a lot of people. I've never heard of him giving away such... sentimental gifts, but I have heard of him doing great things for people. He must *really* like you."

Then, Austin spoke for the first time. "Yeah, I don't know what you did, but, uh...Chin Li's, uh, well, he's an intriguing man." And Austin again let a slight chuckle escape. "Did he quote a bunch of books?"

This statement made Sifu Miller chuckle, and Elliot's suspicion told him that his sifu and sihing was more than acquainted with the old tea master. And with jealousy again flaring up in him, Elliot, with an almost obvious sadness, simply said, "Yeah."

"Yeah, it's always a lesson with him," added Austin with snicker.

Elliot struggled to quell the small flame of jealousy that was flaring up in him. "Why is he just a small tea-shop owner? I mean, from what I get from him and what you're saying, it seems like he could be more successful...or something. I mean, he's got this...worldly, long family history... background. It seems like he could be a famous tea master or even martial arts master. He's clearly got martial arts skill—at least with the sword."

"He's very humble. But don't let that fool you. In the tea world, he *is* very famous. He's actually got a fairly large estate out in Lakeview Heights."

Elliot, shocked by this revelation, interrupted, "Really? He doesn't seem like the kind of person who would live out there."

"Well, you're right. Like I said, he is humble. The property he owns out there is not his house. There are a couple of buildings—teahouses, actually—where he performs tea ceremonies, mostly for rich Asian businessmen, martial artists, and students of tea. People come from all over the world to have him serve them tea, whether it be chanoyu or gung fu tea."

Elliot was further surprised at his sifu's familiarity with tea ceremonies, having never heard his sifu talk about tea. "One building out there is a Japanese teahouse with several tea rooms, and the other structure is more Chinese in architecture. Though, to the untrained eye, like mine, they look the same. And both buildings are surrounded by beautiful landscapes in their respective cultural and traditional styles."

"Have you been out there?"

"Yeah, a couple of times."

This revelation cut Elliot deep, sending his jealously past the breaking point, and as his sifu made this statement, Elliot noticed Austin give a subtle nod, as if he were answering also.

Maybe the old man does serve anybody tea. Maybe he's crazy and doesn't realize he's given away a family heirloom. Why wouldn't he give it to Sifu or somebody like Sifu? He seems more accomplished and deserving than I do.

"Have you ever been to Lakeview?" asked Sifu Miller.

"Oh, huh, what?"

"Lakeview? Have you ever been there?"

"Oh, yeah...I have...well, I've driven around there. I've never had a reason or anyone to visit. Uh, where at in Lakeview? Is it somewhere I can see from the road?"

"No, you can't. It's way out off of the main road through Lakeview—South Lake Drive, actually—but you can't see anything. It's way back, through some woods."

Then Austin added, "Yeah, in fact, the drive is almost hidden. It looks more like a utility or maintenance drive to one of the other estates."

Elliot thought for several moments, trying to imagine just where Chin Li's tea estate and the hidden drive his sihing was describing could be. Sometimes, out of boredom, Elliot would drive around in his car, and he had driven around Lakeview Heights before. *I wonder why Chin Li didn't mention his teahouses. Or that he served tea to people from around the world...that he served tea to Sifu...or Sihing. So much personal family stuff, but nothing about...*

For several moments, Elliot wondered why the tea master hadn't mentioned these things, but mostly, despite his burning jealousy, he wanted to know more about the mysterious and intriguing man. Elliot wondered what other secrets the old man had, and he used his curiosity to get a grip on his jealousy.

Right when Elliot was about to ask his sifu and sihing if they knew anything else about the old man, a knock came from outside the office doorway. They all looked up to a large black man peeking around the door frame into the office. Both Sifu Miller and Sihing Horvath smiled widely as the stranger walked into the crowded office and said hello to them without looking at Elliot. "Joshawn, how's it going?" Sifu asked.

"Good, Sifu. Austin," the man answered as he gave a slight nod to Sihing Horvath. Elliot noted that the man did not address Sihing Horvath by his title. He also noticed that the nod was not really a bow, nor did the man bow to Sifu Miller.

"Ah, Joshawn, I'd like you to meet one of our ranking students, Elliot. Elliot, this is Joshawn. He joined a couple of days ago." Joshawn was large, quite a bit larger than Sifu Miller and Sihing Horvath. The man seemed athletic despite his lack of physical definition. He was light-skinned for an African American, with dark eyes that didn't seem to match his skin tone. His head and face were razor shaved, with razor burn that revealed carelessness. The man looked Elliot up and down for a quick moment before holding out his hand. Elliot did not like the look the new student gave him; it was as if he were sizing Elliot up. He also felt that the new student squeezed his hand too hard while shaking hands. Elliot immediately disliked this newest member of the kwoon.

"Joshawn, we were just talking about, uh, tea, in fact." Sifu Miller said.

Joshawn held his gaze on Elliot for another unnecessary moment before turning to Sifu Miller and responding, "Tea? Who drinks tea? Gimme a real drink. Ya know what I'm sayin'?" and the man scoffed. "Nah, I'm just kiddin'." But Elliot knew he wasn't. "Anyway, Sifu, I was sparrin' around wit' some a' my friends, and I was doin' the jab 'n cross like ya showed me, and I could tell my punches were faster."

And just like that, the conversation went from Elliot's curiosity and unfinished tale of good luck and fortune to

Joshawn. And the curiosity Elliot was using to control his jealousy gave way, except the jealousy was no longer about his sifu, sihing, and Chin Li—it was about Joshawn. Elliot brooded unnoticed as the three other men talked about the jab and cross punch structure, concepts, and principles, not caring that he wanted to know more about Chin Li or that he had met a girl.

Elliot wandered out of the office and into the training area without being acknowledged by the three men, and none of the students waiting in the training area paid attention to him. All of the good feelings he had accumulated over the past couple of days were suddenly gone. But before fear and depression could get a firm grip on him, he thought, *It doesn't matter; that stuff's not as important to them as it is to me. I don't need them to love tea or appreciate the way of the sword. Nor do I need them to know or care about Chrissie. It wouldn't change anything if they did know or care.*

"All right, adults line up." Sihing Horvath lined up the class and warmed them up for training. As Elliot went through the motions, he fought hard not to let his sifu's and sihing's lack of interest get him down. He committed himself to staying positive and looking forward to calling Chrissie. *Yes, Chrissie will change everything.*

It was late in the class when Elliot partnered up with the newest member of the kwoon, Joshawn. Elliot hated the look of contempt Joshawn wore on his face and noticed that the man paused before bowing, as if he was waiting for Elliot to bow first. And when the man finally bowed, it was so slight that it was almost not a bow at all. It was no misunderstanding of etiquette, as Elliot noted how distinctly and correctly the new student bowed to Sifu Miller and the other students. All of Elliot's suspicions were confirmed the minute they touched hands.

They were to be doing simple wrist-escape drills, where one person grabs the other person's wrist while the person being held executes an escape technique. Joshawn, being the newer student, was to grab first. Joshawn was big and strong and gripped Elliot so tightly that Elliot couldn't even begin his technique. Elliot was so immediately frustrated that he couldn't even speak. What would he say? The grabber, the training partner, was supposed to allow a certain level of success for the sake of practice—not complete success, but enough so the student could experience applying the technique in a real sense. Sifu Miller even started the class off with a lecture on training-partner etiquette and how it should be a cooperation, not a competition, and how there should be a 70/30 percent success ratio, meaning at least 30 percent success. But this newest student—who, by all accounts of etiquette, should be showing his senior, his sihing, the utmost respect—was not allowing success or showing cooperation; or respect. *Did he not pay attention? Did he not hear Sifu's words?*

"You know, you're supposed to be allowing *some* success," Elliot finally muttered. Elliot was not far enough in his training to know that the escape starts *before* the opponent has established a firm grip. He just stood there like all of the other students, ignorantly holding out his arm long enough to let his partner, the grabber, cinch a tight grip. Except everyone else's attackers weren't as strong as Elliot's. It was possible to muscle out of a weaker grip, but not Joshawn's.

"Somebody who know how t' 'scape don't need someone t' allow success. I'm da new student. I shouldn't have t' allow *you* success. Ya know what I'm sayin'? You da senior—you should be allowin' *me* success." Joshawn maintained his hold on Elliot's arm. And Elliot hated it—the smirk, the hold, the shaved head, the contempt in his dark eyes, even the way the man wouldn't pronounce or finish his words correctly. It was apparent to Elliot that Joshawn was the epitome of everyone he had ever hated and who had ever hated him throughout school, his various jobs, and now kung fu. Obnoxious, bad etiquette, worse manners, little intelligence, puts forth little effort in life but is liked by everyone and is more successful at everything. *Why does everyone like people like Joshawn... and Marvin? Marvin!*

When it was Elliot's turn to grab Joshawn, he tried to grip Joshawn tightly to prevent the young man from escaping. But Elliot's grip wasn't very strong, and his larger, stronger partner could easily muscle his way out. "You know, that's not the correct technique. If you did it right, you wouldn't be able to get free," Elliot told him.

"I'm gettin' out, ain't I? That's what this exercise is: 'scape, and I'm 'scapin', ain't I? You have t' stop me. So stop me." With a scoff, Joshawn finished, "Ya know?" And he continued to muscle, ignoring form and body mechanics, and Elliot could do nothing about it. Each time Elliot grabbed and Joshawn escaped, Elliot grew angrier, and his partner grew more contemptuous to the point of almost blatant mockery. Joshawn taunted and ridiculed Elliot further as he held his free hand behind his back, as if to suggest he only needed one hand against Elliot.

When class was over, Elliot got changed and gathered his things. All of the students had broken off into little cliques, and Sifu Miller and Sihing Horvath were talking with Joshawn. As Elliot walked by, his sifu and sihing barely looked up as they bowed to him, but Joshawn gave him a long, deliberate look that no one bothered to notice. And the irony of life weighed heavy on Elliot as he contemplated work, where he didn't want to be noticed but was, and kung fu, where he wanted to be noticed but wasn't.

When Elliot got home, he had all but given into despair after the evening's turn of events. His experience with his new *sidai*, his lower-ranking kung fu brother, was almost enough to destroy the newfound happiness and confidence he had acquired over the recent days. But he still had one thing: Chrissie. Elliot had just gotten Chrissie's number the night before, and though he had overheard guys talking about waiting at least three days before calling a girl, he had also, on one occasion, overheard girls talking about liking it when a guy calls the next day. So, mostly out of impatience, Elliot decided to call the next night, which was tonight. Unfortunately, and to his dismay, he got the girl's voice mail.

five

There are commands of the sovereign which must not be obeyed.
—Sun Tzu

Elliot was startled awake by his alarm clock. He felt as if he hadn't slept at all. Back at work, the one place where Elliot wished people would ignore him and leave him alone, he heard jeers and remarks directed at him, but he didn't register what anyone was saying. He just stood at his work-station, waiting for the day to start and time to inevitably stop. "Elliot!" Without having to turn around, Elliot knew that it was his boss, George, and he awaited the coming reprimand for calling in sick the day before. "If you can't get to work, if you can't be here every day, then I'll find somebody who can! Ya got that?" And the short, stout man stormed off. Elliot found this embarrassing and very unnec-essary and tried to remember seeing his boss reprimand any of the other workers as harshly. But he couldn't. The more he thought about it, the more he remembered that other workers, like Marvin, were absent all the time—at least a couple times a month. For a brief moment, Elliot got angry.

Suuuuuck...suuuuuck...suuuuuck...suuuuuck...suuuuuck... suuuuuck...

The relentless, never-ending cycle continued. The next couple of days became another blur in Elliot's life—work was the same, kung fu was the same. He had tried Chrissie a couple of times, leaving his number and a good time to reach him, but she hadn't returned his calls. He had lost all hope and motivation. The exceptional gifts that the generous tea master had bestowed upon him sat lifeless and out of the way. He decided to try Chrissie one last time. Elliot felt that if he could get a hold of her and talk to her, go out with her... *Everything would be better. I know it.*

There was a little voice inside Elliot's head that was telling him Chrissie had been ignoring his calls. As much as he didn't want to believe it, he could not help but be suspicious. He thought the only way he would know if it were true was to call her from a different number or use the *67 service, blocking his number from her caller ID.

"Hello?"

It was true; she must have recognized my number before and not answered. Now that there is no caller ID, she answers.

"Hello?"

"Oh, yeah, sorry, I must have lost you there for a minute. Uh, hi. Hi, it's me, Elliot. We met at WabiCha a few days ago."

"Oh, yeah, how are you?"

"Good. I tried to call a couple times."

"Yeah, I got your messages. I've just...been so busy with school and stuff."

"Oh, it's OK. I understand." There was a long, awkward silence, and Elliot began to panic, not knowing what to say. "Um, so...," and in uncontrollable desperation, he skipped the small talk and blurted out, "You want to get together sometime? Maybe get drinks somewhere...or, uh, dinner or something?"

"Uh, yeah...that'd...that'd be...great. I'm kinda busy the next couple of weeks, though...with school and stuff, but, uh...give me a call sometime."

Elliot detected a distinct tone in her voice when she said "give me a call sometime." It was so subtle but hit him like ice-cold water. There was another long pause, and Elliot knew this was good-bye. What else was there to say? There was finality in her voice, which made it clear to Elliot that she was saying good-bye for good, with no intention of going out with him. *"Call me sometime." What did that mean? When is sometime?*

"Uh, yeah, OK. I can do that. I'll call you...sometime...say, in the next week or two."

"OK, great. Well, I gotta get going. It was good talking to you. I'll see you 'round." And she hung up almost before Elliot could respond.

"Yeah, OK, see ya 'round."

Whatever that means.

* * *

Tonight was a training night for Elliot, but he did not want to go. He was still feeling bad about being blown off by Chrissie. He really feared that Sifu Miller would see right through him and ask him what was wrong, and he certainly didn't want to talk about it. But mostly he feared Joshawn and his over-bearing contempt, and he knew he couldn't handle it. When Elliot got home from work, he called his sifu.

"Hello, Shaolin Academy."

"Yeah, Sifu? Uh..."

"Yes, Elliot, how are you?"

"Uh, yeah, Sifu, how are you? I don't think I'm going to make it in tonight."

"Oh, why not? Is everything all right?"

Elliot gave his usual excuse. "Oh, yeah! Everything's fine. I just, uh, I gotta get up early tomorrow. We, uh, we're doing overtime, and I have to be in early." As soon as he was done speaking, he felt a sudden shame, as he always did, for lying. This was not the first time he had called his sifu and used this excuse, and lying always made him feel terrified of being caught. He was always sure that Sifu knew he was lying, but his teacher never questioned him.

"OK. Well...maybe come in for just a minute? We could chat a little."

"I don't know, Sifu. Maybe. I really—"

"Just for a few minutes. I'd like to see you. I feel like I didn't get to hear the rest of your story the other day. It seems like I haven't really seen much of you lately."

There was a long pause as Elliot tried to summon the courage to just say no. But Elliot was drawing a blank. Sifu Miller broke the young man's concentration. "Come on...just for a few minutes."

And Elliot, folding under the pressure, finally agreed. "OK, I'll stop in for a minute. It might be a little later, though." Elliot thought that if he went in during the middle of class, Sifu Miller would not want to step away from training for too long, so Elliot would not be stuck there any longer than he had to be.

After Elliot got off the phone, he desperately tried to think of something to do. He couldn't bear the thought of lying on his sofa again. Elliot had spent the past couple of evenings lying on his sofa, staring at the ceiling until his apartment grew dark. Although he tried hard to think of something, anything, to do, nothing appealed to him— nothing except WabiCha Teahouse. Despite his current state of depression, he had an overwhelming desire to be near people—anyone except his coworkers and his *sipai*, his kung fu family. He certainly had no desire to talk to people; he just didn't want to be alone. And though he feared running into the tea-shop owner, he could think of nowhere else to go where he could sit and be near people without being too out of place. With a little reluctance, he chose to go to WabiCha.

When Elliot got to the tea salon, he requested to sit at the window. Typically, he would be glad to sit closer to the back in the hope of being noticed by the owner. But today, Elliot was hoping for the opposite. He did not want to see Chin Li any more than he did his sifu or anyone else he knew. Elliot also had no desire to read, which was his usual routine. And because he thought he would feel more awkward staring at an open book and pretending to read or looking around the tiny teahouse, he opted to stare out the window. As Elliot sat in front of the window, making and sipping his tea, he slowly watched the cars drive by. He tried to guess what people did for a living by the clothes they were wearing and the type and condition of vehicles they were driving. This is something Elliot did often, whether he was looking out a window somewhere, driving in his own car, or walking. He always watched people in their cars. What he was really looking for was to see if the people appeared happy or not. Elliot had long felt that people who were driving alone in their vehicles showed their true feelings. A car sheltered a person and had a way of making one feel comfortable, secure, detached, and forgetful of the world outside. Almost hypnotically, people would take off their masks and reveal their true selves, unaware that the outside world, if it were at all interested, could see in.

For most of his life, Elliot had assumed that people were generally happy, and the better careers and more money people had, all the more happy they were. But since he began making his observations, he couldn't help but notice that many people seemed unhappy. Whether a person had nice clothes and a nice car or cheap clothes and cheap car—poor, rich, clean, dirty—it didn't matter. Some people seemed happy, and some people did not. This revelation should be good for someone who thinks he's the only and most unhappy person on the planet, but for Elliot, it made him all the more depressed. The thought that even money and a successful career could fail to bring happiness made Elliot sadder.

"Ah, it is young Maste' Elliot. How a'e you?"

Chin Li's sudden greeting from behind startled Elliot, as it usually did, and when he turned around, the tea master was rising up from a bow. Elliot, awkward from the sudden surprise, bowed back and replied, "Uh, Master Chin, I'm good. How are you?"

"Ah, you not 'ead tonight, Maste' Elliot." This was more of an observation than a question.

"Uh...oh, yeah, I...I'm just tired...not really in the mood tonight." Elliot was struggling to find words.

"How is iaido and gung fu tea?"

Elliot was immediately embarrassed. He thought for sure that the wise old tea master would be able to tell he had not been practicing. Elliot felt ashamed for not using or appreciating the gifts. "Uh...yeah, I mean, yeah. I did...have been. I mean I did the first night, but, uh, I've been real busy at work and...well, just work. Lots of overtime. It's hard to find time with all the overtime." Elliot could not look Chin Li in the eye. He was not only ashamed for not using the gifts but for lying about having to work overtime and being busy. Elliot was sure that, like his sifu, the wise old tea master could tell he was lying.

Chin Li was not offended or perplexed. The tea master casually said, "Ah, yes, wo'k. That just life, Elliot. Sometime life get in way. Life is balance. Balance wo'k, balance t'aining, balance f'iend and family. Sometime scale go one way, then othe'."

Elliot had to make a conscious effort to resist Chin Li's warm smile. *Yeah, friends and family!* While Chin Li was speaking, Elliot, as subtly as he could, was getting up and preparing to leave. By the time Chin Li finished speaking, Elliot was ready to go but wasn't sure how to respond to the tea master. "Uh...yeah, balance. Well, right now the scale is on the work side. And speaking of work...I gotta get up early tomorrow, so...as much as I'd love to stay and chat...I should really be going." Elliot slowly and casually walked past Chin Li.

"Oh, OK, Maste' Elliot. You go get sleep. I see you soon." And the old man waved and bowed slightly.

Elliot was overwhelmed with shame and embarrassment. He quickly returned the bow to the tea master, turned, and rushed out.

* * *

Elliot walked into the kwoon while there was a class in session. He walked casually behind the class, trying not to make eye contact with anyone, certain that everyone's looks would be searching—judging. Elliot could not help but glance up at Sifu Miller and Sihing Horvath as their eyes bored into him. And it was also proper etiquette upon entering a kwoon to bow at the door and then wait to be recognized by the sifu so as to bow to the sifu and seniors. So Elliot could not ignore these stares that penetrated deeply into him. These were not ordinary stares. People often stared at Elliot, but these were not stares of disgust or discontent. These stares were different. Elliot had seen these looks on his sifu and his sihing before, and recently he had seen a similar look on Chin Li's face. But these looks always confused Elliot. By all accounts, they seemed hostile, but Elliot was sure they were not. He knew there had been no intended hostility the times he had seen his sifu with this look, usually during class or a lecture. Sihing Horvath...*Well, his might be hostile. I can never tell with him.* And finally there was Chin Li. Elliot could not imagine the old tea master getting hostile with anyone, only occasional sternness. *Why would they give me hostile looks?* No, these looks weren't hostile. However, every time someone looked at Elliot this way, it made him want to look away. Elliot quickly bowed to his sifu and sihing, who, with the imposing stares, promptly returned the bow.

"Elliot, go ahead and wait in the office. I'll be right there." Sifu Miller turned his attention back to the class. Elliot didn't wait to listen or hear what Sifu Miller was lecturing about. He just hurried back to the office, hoping his sifu would not take long or want to talk for long. To his relief, Sifu Miller appeared at the office door moments later and said, "Sorry about that." He then walked over to his desk chair, sat down across from Elliot, and said, "Just wanted to finish my thought." To Elliot's further relief, Sifu Miller's mysterious look was gone, but the one that replaced it was just as penetrating. There was a long pause, and though Sifu Miller's present look was much softer than his earlier one, Elliot could still not hold eye contact.

"How's work? All the overtime must be exhausting. Good money, though," he said, trying to start the conversation on a positive note, overlooking that Elliot was lying about overtime.

Even though the overtime was a lie, extra overtime money had never meant anything to Elliot. He always appreciated the time off far more and always hated when people would say things like that to him. To Elliot, money, especially overtime money, was an excuse, almost a lie, people would tell themselves in an attempt to convince themselves that work was tolerable or OK—even acceptable. *How can anyone accept his or her job? Even for more money.* Elliot had always felt that normal workdays took up so much of a person's life that to give more time was an infringement of what little freedom was left. It was like prison that let you go home in the evenings to sleep in your own bed. But if they wanted to make you stay longer, they could.

Yes, Elliot hated it when people made these kinds of statements, and he felt a sudden deep hostility spark in him upon hearing Sifu Miller, *his* sifu, try and trick him into accepting his job. Before he could stop himself, Elliot blurted out, "I don't care about the money, Sifu. I hate overtime. I hate normal time. I hate any time at work."

There was a short intentional pause as Sifu Miller processed Elliot's sudden and definitive statement. Elliot had such finality in his tone that Sifu Miller was momentarily unsure what to say. He knew it was imperative to change Elliot's way of thinking in terms of work but feared it might be too late. Elliot obviously had a deep-seated hatred for his job and had already decided to never love, like, or even accept it. The wise teacher thought for a brief moment about suggesting that Elliot find a different job, but his experience told him that people with this mind-set just go from job to job with the same attitude. "So, Elliot, tell me again, what is it exactly that you hate so much about your job?"

Again, unable to control his reaction, Elliot scoffed and said, "What's not to hate? I hate the people, the bosses, the work..." Elliot wanted to say more but could think of nothing. He could feel the hostility growing in him and again felt offended at his sifu's obvious attempt to guide him to a more accepting attitude about work.

Pressing on, Sifu Miller continued. "Well, Elliot, I understand. The people—"

Growing more unable to control himself, Elliot cut in, "No, Sifu, you don't. You don't understand!"

Patiently, Sifu Miller held up a hand, gesturing for Elliot to stop. "Wait, just wait. Let me finish. I'm sorry. You're right. I can't know how it is for you. But I am familiar with people that are not easy to get along with, whether it's coworkers or bosses or both. And I've had jobs I didn't particularly like."

Elliot could feel nothing but anger burning in him, like a fire growing hotter and hotter. The more his sifu talked, the hotter the fire was getting, and Elliot could barely control it. He believed that his sifu had known and maybe even had worked with difficult people before, but it couldn't have been anything like what Elliot was dealing with. If his sifu understood what Elliot was going through, Elliot was sure that he would be giving him different advice. Elliot was certain that Sifu Miller would tell him to demand more respect from his coworkers. He even imagined his sifu, in these extreme circumstances, coaching him on fighting some of his coworkers to get respect.

Sifu Miller continued. "Elliot, like I've been saying, *you* have to find the good. You have to make the job yours. Take pride in what you do, no matter how menial the task may be—"

At this, Elliot could control his anger no longer. "Sifu, you've never worked in a factory!" Elliot only assumed this, and he was right. Sifu Miller had never worked in manufacturing. "You want me to take pride in my job, but I do one thing—one measly little thing!" And he held up his index finger, all his muscles tense. Suppressing his shouts, but not his anger, Elliot went on, forgetting about etiquette. "I stick a tube in a dead turkey's ass! Anyone can do it. You can't find pride in that. All of the guts get ripped out anyway; you don't even need to do that job. They've processed the turkeys all day long without a shit sucker when they've been shorthanded. I couldn't fuck that job up! How do I do it better? How do I go home convincing myself that I did that job better than anyone else?" Elliot had rarely cursed in his life, and never at anyone. The tone and language he heard himself use surprised him so much that the hostility momentarily subsided.

Further surprised at Elliot's growing hostility and contempt, Sifu Miller waited a moment after Elliot spoke, hoping the young man was calming down a bit. Before the teacher could speak, Elliot spoke again, except this time with an almost pleading tone. "Sifu, imagine doing something that simple." And Elliot looked at a half-empty bottle of water on the desk. "Take your water bottle. Imagine taking the cap and screwing it on. Now imagine doing it over and over. Not taking it off, just putting it on, nothing else. Once you put that cap on, you do it to the next bottle, and then the next, and the next..." Elliot's speech slowed down, and his hostility, almost as suddenly as it had come, ceased. "At first, you do take a little pride in it. You can put on as many caps as anyone else, and before long, you can put on more. And even though it hurts your hands, you do a little extra every day. All of your coworkers, who are already mean to you, are shittier now because you're making them look bad to the bosses. And the bosses, they don't ever say anything to you. No 'good job' or 'well done' or 'keep it up.' No, they only speak to your coworkers. 'Why aren't you doing as many as him? Why aren't doing more?' Pretty soon, based on only *your* performance, the bosses decide that everybody's numbers should go up. 'If he can do that many, everyone should be able to.' So if your coworkers hated you before, now they really hate you. But that's not the worst part. They also raise your numbers, even though you were already exceeding your rate. Now, not only can your coworkers not make rate, but neither can you. So your coworkers hate you and give you a hard time, and now your bosses are on your back all the time, wondering why you aren't making rate any longer. They don't care that that you used to make rate plus some." There was a long pause before Elliot finished. "You're only as good as today's numbers."

Elliot came out of his stupor to find Sifu Miller staring at him. Even though Sifu Miller still felt compelled to reason with Elliot, he was at a loss for words. Sifu Miller knew Elliot wasn't referring to his present job, but a culmination of all his jobs. What could he say to that? Although Elliot could still feel the hostility deep inside him, he suddenly felt in control. He was sure that his sifu didn't understand and was confident that he never would. Accepting this fact, Elliot no longer felt offended at his sifu's attempts to help him. Calmly, Elliot interrupted the silence. "Sifu, I *do* understand what you're trying to tell me—all that about loving your job. I know that if I loved my job, they would have no power over me. I know it's my choice. My work... I mean the soulless, faceless being... the power that it is... wants me to love my job, too. Imagine a worker who never complains and does what he's told no matter what. Like a soldier. 'Tis not but to reason why...' I grasp that concept more than you know. But I can't love my job. I can't. Then they'll have me."

Sifu Miller was looking at Elliot with perplexity. He was trying to understand his student. Elliot could tell his sifu was struggling to understand, but Elliot was not sure how to effectively convey why he couldn't possibly love his job. Then Elliot thought of something. "You know, there are some older people at work—people who have been there for years and years. When they come back from a vacation or any length of time off, you know what they say? They say things like, 'I enjoyed the time off, but, boy, am I glad to be back.' Glad to be back?"

Elliot suddenly felt a sense of shock, as if this was the first time he had heard someone, even himself, make this statement. "How can anyone...why would anyone be glad? And if you look into their eyes, there's an emptiness. These people don't have hobbies or other things—no life outside of work, just work. They've given in and given everything else up. These are the people who truly love overtime. They *love* being at work. They're dead inside, Sifu, and they *love* their jobs." Still in a half-hypnotic state, Elliot looked directly at his sifu and said, "No, Sifu, I will not love my job, no matter the misery that entails."

* * *

After Elliot left the kwoon, he went home. He could still feel the hostility in him, but he also felt an odd sense of control. Although he had always been determined to not love his job, saying it out loud brought a certain sense of closure. This closure was allowing the self-control to flow through him. Control was something else that Elliot was not familiar with. His whole life, he had been afraid to make decisions, which often led him to make bad decisions. There was no doubt in his mind that all of his bad decisions had led him to this place in life. His decisions to do poorly in school and not go to college, along with his social anxieties, made it virtually impossible for him to find more fulfilling work, to meet people and make friends...to meet women. But now he felt a sense of control, and he chose not to question it.

When Elliot got home, he lay on the sofa, but he didn't feel bad about it. He lay there uncharacteristically comfortably and thought about the past few days. And his recollection of those days began to blur and become black as he drifted into an almost unconscious state. He saw himself drifting through the days like he had been his whole life—like a ghost. No one spoke to him, and he spoke to no one. Drifting from home to job to home. He *was* a ghost.

Elliot awoke, feeling numb and empty but not in his usual painful, depressed way. Not sad but not happy either, just numb—stoic. Feeling a desire to just sit and drink tea and watch television all day, Elliot called in sick to work and, to his surprise, felt no guilt whatsoever. And that's exactly what he did all day: drank tea and watched the same old movies he'd been watching for years. Typically, the thought of watching one of his old movies again would depress him further, as he had seen them so many times, but not today. Today, he was perfectly content.

By midafternoon, Elliot started to think about his sifu and kung fu. He began to feel ashamed for lying to his sifu and breaching etiquette by shouting and cussing in his sifu's presence. Then his thoughts drifted to his physical training. He had always struggled with his inability to acquire physical skills. Since he had begun kung fu, this inability had had a demoralizing impact on his training and heavily contributed to his overall depression. *Why do I even go? Isn't work bad enough? Do I really need to add more stress to my life? Even work would be easier without kung fu. I mean, I spend most of my days dreading kung fu, making my workdays longer and harder. What is kung fu doing for me anyway, except making my life harder?*

Ring...ring...ring...ring...ring...

The ringing phone interrupted Elliot's thoughts. It was Sifu Miller. When Elliot answered the phone, both men were surprised to hear the other's voice. Sifu Miller was surprised because he thought Elliot would be at work and was calling to leave a message on the answering machine. Elliot was surprised because he assumed his sifu might be upset with him due to his behavior.

"Elliot, I didn't think you'd be home. I was just going to leave you a message to call me."

"Yeah, well, I didn't feel like going in today." After a short pause, Elliot continued, "Sifu, I'm sorry I got mad yesterday and yelled—"

Sifu Miller cut Elliot off. "Elliot, Elliot, it's all right. I understand. I wanted to talk to you because I wanted to apologize. You're right. I have never worked in a factory, and I'm sorry for misunderstanding or misinterpreting the depth of...how bad work is for you. And for that, I'm sorry. But if I may say one more thing on the subject, then I'll say no more."

Elliot didn't say anything. He was not expecting his sifu to apologize to him. This made him feel guiltier for being disrespectful and for contemplating quitting kung fu.

After a brief pause, Sifu Miller went on. "I will tell you, from one warrior to another, that the battlefield is different for everyone. For some, the battlefield is literal, and the enemy is obvious—the objectives are obvious. For the rest of us, the battle lines are not so defined. The enemies are not so clear. For some, the battlefield is out there!" Sifu Miller put emphasis on "out there," and Elliot could sense Sifu Miller thrusting his finger in the air, as if pointing to some battlefield off in the distance.

"Some soldiers, they go through battles, and even wars, without having to do any fighting—no struggle. And then there are some, it seems, who do all of the fighting. Some soldiers, some warriors, they choose it that way. The rest, no matter how hard they try or how hard they choose, it doesn't matter. It's chosen for them. But a warrior, a true warrior, doesn't complain or give up. That's what makes him a warrior. Whether behind a desk or on the front lines, in the trenches, he just does it."

Sifu Miller's speech was making Elliot feel even guiltier. He knew his sifu was right. Ironically, though, it did not make Elliot change his mind about wanting to quit kung fu. Nor did it make him feel any more like a warrior. It made him feel not like a warrior at all.

"And, Elliot, not to sound melodramatic, but it seems to me as if you're in the trenches. You're in the thick of it, and right now you can't get out. All you can do is get up every day, dig in, and keep fighting. Love it or hate it, you just *can't* give up; giving up is death. Those people you talked about, the empty ones, they're dead; they gave up. Are you going to walk through the rest of your life dead?"

There was a long pause. Elliot wasn't sure what to say or how to say it. He understood what his sifu was saying and agreed; he was in the trenches. And put in that perspective, Elliot was able to accept his fate just a little bit. But kung fu was something he didn't have to accept or tolerate, and he still felt an overwhelming urge to quit. "Sifu, you're right. I've never thought of it that way, but deep down I've always known it. I know I have to just keep going. It's just sometimes..."

"Elliot, you don't need to explain yourself. Life is relative. What's hard for some is not hard for others. And what's hard for others is not hard for some. But life gets hard for everyone, and I mean *everyone*. Sometimes you just gotta let it out, and that's OK." After a short pause, Sifu Miller continued. "Why don't you come to class tonight and take your mind off work?"

And here was the moment Elliot had been waiting for. He knew his sifu was going to ask him to go to class. The hostility toward his sifu gone and the love for him back in full measure, Elliot suddenly wanted to be near his teacher. But his dread for training had taken over his emotions.

"Sifu, I get what you're saying about work and all that stuff; I really do. But I'm not feeling kung fu. I don't think I'm cut out for it." Elliot was speaking a little faster than usual in an attempt to say all he had to say and not allow his sifu to cut in. "I'm not getting the physical applications. Sometimes I don't understand the concepts. I'm not really making any friends or identifying with anyone. It stresses me out. I spend my day stressed out about training, and it makes my day at work even harder to deal with. I don't need that. I get what you're saying about work being war and all that, and I need to stay focused if I'm going to make it through. I don't need another war or battle or whatever that I can't win."

Sifu Miller was not surprised. Kung fu had a high student turnover, and most students quit around this time in their training. Especially students with dispositions like Elliot's. "Well, Elliot, I hear exactly what you're saying, and I understand why you think that. But let me tell you, as your sifu, you are wrong. You *are* getting it—"

Elliot, assuming that Sifu Miller gave this speech to everyone who wanted to quit and feeling slightly offended at the very notion, cut in. "No, I'm not, Sifu! I've been training for months and months, and people who started around the time I did are way better than me. And then we get new people who just start, and I can't even handle them!"

"Elliot, you can't compare yourself to others. You can only compare yourself to yourself. Everyone is at a different place in their training and in their lives. And I, as a sifu, only hold people to their individual standards. Everyone is diff—"

"Sifu, I'm just not getting it. I—"

"Elliot, you *are* getting it. When you started, you were so timid that you would barely do the exercises during warm-up. And to ask you a question in class? You would completely freeze up; you wouldn't speak. You couldn't even look at me or whoever asked the question. And now...and now you sometimes line up the class and take them through warm-ups."

Elliot scoffed slightly. He didn't want to accept that Sifu Miller was right about the confidence he had gained, however little it seemed. "Sifu, that's not what I mean. I can't get the physical—"

"But it is the same. It is. Your confidence is reflected in your physical application. When you started, it was like you were afraid to hit people and afraid to get hit. And now I see you going through the drills and trying—I mean really trying. Your confidence might not be where you want, but it is progressing."

There was a pause. Elliot was deep in thought, trying to resist the truth of what his sifu was telling him.

Sifu Miller continued, "It's true that some students progress quicker—some at physical, some at mental, some at both—"

"But, Sifu, I can't stand the fact that we get new students who are already better than me!"

"Like I said, you shouldn't compare yourself to others, especially him. I know who you're referring to." Sifu Miller paused for a moment as he searched for the words. Elliot could hear his sifu start to talk and stop a couple of times, and Elliot knew that he was struggling with what to say next. "It's bad etiquette for me—or us—to talk about another student, about Joshawn, but I will say this: Joshawn is athletic, and he's got a little street-fighting experience, and, as you know, experience goes a long way. His athletic abilities, his attributes, and his fighting experience will carry him. For a little way, anyway. But there is a limit to that. People with his background, or similar to it, fall into traps. They get the basics right away, and even excel in them. But the concepts and more complex techniques take them way longer than other students.

"Students like you—who have no martial arts background, who have no fighting experience—might take longer getting the basics, but you're a clean slate, a blank canvas. You have no preconceived notions about what a punch is or what a kick is, so later on, when we introduce you to complex advanced techniques, you will not question them. Your body karma will not resist so much. Students like Joshawn, who have had success with basic kicking and punching, will always rely on basic kicking and punching. When they're introduced to advanced techniques that don't work for them at first, and they never do at first, they fall back to what's worked for them. They never fully experience advanced concepts because they always go back to what they know. And when they face someone who understands advanced concepts and techniques..."

Sifu didn't even finish his last sentence; he didn't have to. He could tell by the ensuing silence that Elliot knew what he was saying. "Besides, Elliot, all this physical...stuff, for lack of a better word, it's low-level kung fu. Even the highest physical skill is low-level kung fu—a by-product of what kung fu really is, and that's character development. That's the point I was initially trying to make. And your development has come a long way. You should not give up now."

Finally giving in and accepting the truth of his sifu's words, Elliot felt that he couldn't quit, even though he still felt an urge to. With reluctance, Elliot said, "OK, Sifu, you're right. I'll be in."

"Tonight?"

"Uh, I don't know about tonight. Maybe..."

"It's gotta be tonight, Elliot. The fight is right now. Not tomorrow, not next week...*right now*."

Elliot felt that he couldn't say no, no matter how much he wanted to, so with even more reluctance, he agreed. "OK, OK, Sifu, I'll be in tonight."

* * *

Elliot really didn't want go to kung fu, but deep down, he knew his sifu was right; if he couldn't make it on this night, he would not be able to make himself go ever again. However, there was one thing that was helping him get to class, and that was the idea that he would see his sifu. He felt closure about being disrespectful to his teacher, and he felt good about the sincerity his sifu displayed in wanting him to return to class. But, to his utter disappointment, Sifu Miller was absent. Sihing Horvath was running classes, and all he said about Sifu Miller's absence was, "Sifu had to step out for the evening." This sent Elliot's spirits spiraling down. Elliot spent the first half of class distracted by his internal struggle to regain the stoic attitude he'd had earlier in the day and bring his morale back up. It was not until he partnered up with his new nemesis, Joshawn, that his focus was brought back to class.

"All right, we're going to do recovery-from-the-takedown drills. You're going to let your partner put his leg behind yours and give you a little push, and *without* resisting, you are going to fall, using your break-fall technique; establish space; and get your hands and feet where they need to be: between you and your partner. We are not practicing the takedown or the anti-takedown, so if you're the attacker, just give a little push for a stimulus, and victim, you are *not* resisting the takedown, so when you feel that push, fall down."

Sihing Horvath had more of an authoritative way of teaching, with an almost punisher-type mentality. He would sometimes raise his voice to regain control of a class that got out of hand, and he ran a lot of drills, much like a drill sergeant in the military. He had developed these character-istics from his retired military father, his own short time in the military, and his past harsh martial arts training. The middle-aged teacher was also slightly broad shouldered and very physically defined, with an older style flattop buzz cut that completed the militant look. All of these characteristics, along with the man's usual intense glare, known in American military lore as the thousand-yard stare, made Sihing Austin Horvath a very imposing figure. Sihing Horvath was very much in contrast to Sifu Miller, who had a more subtle way of teaching and a way of managing the class to a point where the class ran itself and he just monitored.

Even when it came to changing partners, Sihing Horvath was very specific and direct about what he wanted and how he wanted it, giving everyone unnecessary instructions. Sifu Miller had been training and guiding the teacher toward the sifu's style of teaching, but when Sifu Miller was absent, Sihing Horvath digressed to his punisher ways. "All right, bow to your partner and begin."

Elliot bowed to his partner, who scarcely returned the ges-ture. Determined to resist Joshawn's seemingly intentional attempt to disrespect him, Elliot ignored his partner's contempt. Joshawn immediately took charge. "You push me first," he said, and though etiquette dictated that the sidai, the junior, give the stimulus first, Elliot didn't argue. Elliot reached back with his right leg and put it behind his partner's legs, put his hands on the larger man's chest, and gave a light push. But instead of falling down, Joshawn stiffened up and gave a subtle push with his chest. Since Elliot was on one leg and reaching out with the other, he was off balance, and the slight push from his partner caused him to lose the rest of his balance, stumble, and fall down.

Suddenly, there was an explosion of light that blinded Elliot. The explosion sent a shock wave through his body, and the light was so bright that it took him a moment to realize what was going on and where he was. It was not unconsciousness that seized him; it was anger—cold, hard anger—something that Elliot had never fully experienced before. The blinding light dissipated, and the determination he was holding on to so tightly was gone, and Elliot lay on the mat, looking up at a mocking, condescending grin that had haunted him his whole life—on the faces of his schoolmates, his coworkers, on strangers. After a moment of laying there and looking up, Elliot suddenly felt as if he were no longer in his body. It was as if he were suddenly outside, looking down at a weak and wretched person who was useless and unnecessary. And then there was another explosion, but this was different.

In that moment of time, something happened that Elliot could barely believe. He sprang up from the ground and screamed, "What the fuck is your problem?" and struck Joshawn in the jaw, instantly knocking the larger man unconscious. "You think you're so fucking big, don't you? Huh? Always fucking with the little guy, the weak guy. I bet you've never tried to fuck with somebody bigger, have you? *Have you*?" He kicked the unconscious body hard in the ribs. "Now who looks like the idiot? Now who looks like the pussy?" Then Elliot looked up and around, fists still clenched tight.

Everyone was frozen, staring in shock and disbelief. But Sihing Horvath wasn't. He was staring, but his look was different from everyone else's. It was that same intense, mysterious look that bore into him. The look he had seen on his sihing and sifu before; the look he had even seen on his friend, the tea master, Chin Li. But this time, Elliot wasn't trying to figure the look out. He didn't care, and after several moments of standing there, he stormed out, ignoring Sihing Horvath's unwavering stare and everyone else's gawking.

Time was moving quickly, and Elliot didn't have the chance or desire to replay what had happened. It seemed so long ago, but it had only been moments. He was still in an uncontrolled state and had the feeling of watching himself from without. He had never experienced such a tempest of emotion. When he got home, almost as if someone else were controlling him, he violently shoved things out of his way, got out his katana, and began drawing his blade and shouting "kiai!" With every shout came an explosion and shock wave of emotion that scared the Elliot on the outside looking in. "Kiai...kiai...kiai...kiai..."

Pound, pound, pound...

The muffled voice of Elliot's neighbor Drew echoed through the wall. "Hey, Elliot! Shut the fuck up over there! Some of us gotta work in the morning!"

But that did not stop Elliot. The Elliot on the outside heard the voice, but not the Elliot with the sword. "Kiai...kiai...kiai... kiai..."

Pound, pound, pound...

"Hey! You want me to fucking come over there? Keep it down!"

If the storm that was Elliot had subsided at all, it now returned in full force. Elliot slashed the wall and then thrust his blade through it, shouting, "Yeah, come the fuck over here, and we'll see who keeps it down! So, fuck you! *You* keep it down!" Then Elliot jerked the sword from the wall, releasing chunks of plaster with it, took a couple of deep breaths, and continued drawing and cutting.

Drew was looking at the hole left by Elliot's sword thrust and, out of shock and fear, apologized just loud enough for Elliot to hear. "OK, Elliot. It's OK. Sorry. You go ahead and shout as loud as you want."

But Elliot didn't register the apology. He just kept drawing, cutting, and shouting, "Kiai...kiai...kiai...kiai..."

six

It was daylight when Elliot finally woke. He had stayed up practicing iaido well into the night. He was no longer in a state of uncontrollable, blinding rage. Even after realizing he had forgot to set his alarm and that he was nearly two hours late for work, he didn't panic or stress out as he would have in the past. He just continued to lay there, embracing a sense of freedom he couldn't define in words.

Elliot arrived at work just after first break, and instead of reporting to his immediate supervisor, as was proper proce- dure, he wandered through the plant somewhat aimlessly, in a roundabout way, toward his workstation. He was oblivious to the stares and looks of surprise from his coworkers, who seemed to be wondering why quiet little Elliot was wandering around the plant. "Elliot! What the fuck? Ya called in to work again, and now you're comin' t' work late, and ya don't call... that's considered a 'no-call.' I could fire ya for that! If ya can't make it t' work or be here on time, I'll find somebody who can!"

Elliot calmly turned to face his boss, George, who was standing there, short and hostile. Elliot stared at the man for a long, tense moment without saying or doing anything. He noticed a slight unease creep over the stocky little man as Elliot continued to calmly stare at him. Then Elliot stepped close to his supervisor and, in a low, hostile voice, said, "Yeah, you go ahead and do that. If you wanna fire me, go right ahead. If you think you can find somebody who'll stand there all day every day and suck shit like I do, go ahead." Elliot got even closer to his supervisor's face and thrust his finger at the now intimidated man. "But good luck finding somebody who'll tolerate it as much as *I-fucking-have*!"

George casually backed away from Elliot and stuttered as he tried to find words. "O...O...OK, Elliot, you...you...you're right. Everybody's late once in a while. It's OK. You...you just...uh, you just go ahead and do what you gotta do ta...ta... get ready, and when you're done or...whatever, you just go t' your station. All right? All right." And the plump little man let out an unintentional sigh of relief as he saw the hostility drain from his young employee.

Though Elliot felt hostility when he spoke to his boss, it wasn't an all-consuming, blinding rage, and it abated immediately upon his boss's reply. The two men stood there in silence for a moment. Then Elliot gave a slight shrug of indifference before turning and walking away. He did not need to do anything else to get ready, nor did he desire to wander around any longer. So he went directly to his workstation and, without apology, relieved the person who was covering for him.

Elliot was, as usual, fully aware of the time, but for once in his life, he didn't care. He couldn't hear the pounding of the clock, and he decided he wouldn't care if he did. And for a moment, he realized that time wasn't dragging like usual, nor was it speeding by like it had as of late. It was moving normally. But only for a moment did he care to observe the pace of time before he gave way back to apathy.

At lunchtime, Elliot unconsciously headed toward the restroom in the back of his department. Even though this restroom was quite a bit out of the way, Elliot often chose it because hardly anyone else did. Typically, he was trying to avoid people—hiding from the torment that his coworkers could not resist inflicting on him. But this time it was out of sheer habit, as his apathy left him in a state of unconscious action, with his body drifting through the motions. Elliot turned down the long, narrow, secluded hallway that led to the restroom.

"Well, well, if it isn't the part-timer. Must be nice to get t' come t' work whenever ya want."

Without turning around, Elliot knew who it was. He could tell it was Marvin by the nasal, whiny voice and sarcastic tone that was so characteristic of the malicious man. Elliot didn't even turn around. He simply thought to himself, *What a piece of shit. He misses work all the time, and he wants to give me shit for missing a couple of days. And now he's going to say something about me being gay because he can't think of anything new or better to say.* Sensing the man walk right up behind him, Elliot stopped walking and emptied his mind of thought.

"Comin' in late, walkin' around...you must really be gettin' your knees dirty with the boss." Then Marvin kneed Elliot hard, right on the tailbone, and said, "Is that it, faggot?"

Elliot found himself standing over the man. There was no blinding light or storm of emotion, no out-of-body experience like the night before with his sidai, just a lapse in consciousness, as if he had skipped a moment in time. Marvin was starting to sit up and look around, mumbling as he slowly regained his ability to speak. Elliot said nothing. He just turned and proceeded into the restroom.

When he got into the restroom, he caught himself in the mirror. His blank expression was so unfamiliar that he almost didn't recognize himself at first glance. Then, as he regained his own consciousness, the seriousness of the situation set in, and Elliot felt a panic rise in him. Not of Marvin coming into the restroom and starting more trouble, but of Marvin running and telling the bosses. Although Elliot hated his job with an indescribable passion, he hated finding a new job even more. The thought of interviews with strangers and answering questions and talking about himself always brought on an overwhelming sense of fear and anxiety. And now, he was sure he was going to have to do it again. Elliot stood in front of the mirror and stared at his own blank expression for a long time as his feelings, to his surprise, teetered between panic and his newfound apathy before he accepted the inevitability of his situation. Realizing that he had stood there for his entire twenty-minute lunch break, he calmly walked out into the deserted hallway and made his way back to his workstation just in time for the line to start. All he could do was wait.

It was just before last break when George and George's immediate boss, Tony, the facilitator, came and got Elliot. To his surprise, he felt no fear or embarrassment at being singled out by the bosses or stared at by all his coworkers. The three men walked along the assembly line to a catwalk that led up to the offices. When the three men filed into the small, empty conference room at the top of the catwalk stairs, Marvin was already waiting. To Elliot's further surprise, Marvin had a shocked look on his face. Marvin and Elliot continued to look at each other in confusion as everyone sat down. There was a long pause as Elliot and Marvin held each other's gaze.

Their gaze was finally broken when Tony spoke. "Well, gentlemen, I'm sure you know why you're here." It was obvious by his appearance and the way he conducted himself that Tony was middle management. Whereas George was short and plump with thinning, greasy hair, a thick mustache, large bifocals, dingy jeans, and an old plaid button-up work shirt, Tony was tall and clean-cut, with nice dress pants, a dress shirt, and a tie. *I bet he's never even worked out on the floor or on the line.* And Elliot hated him for it.

Both Elliot and Marvin looked backed at each other, their uncertainty and suspicion deepening. Tony and George looked at the two men, one and then the other, before Tony went on, not waiting any longer for a reply from the two employees. "It has been brought to our attention that you both were engaged in a physical confrontation today."

Again Elliot and Marvin looked at each other searchingly, suspiciously. It began to appear to Elliot that maybe Marvin didn't tell. *If Marvin didn't tell, who did?*

"Well? What do you have to say for yourselves?"

Elliot looked back to his bosses, and both of them were staring at him. *Well, this is it. They both know I punched Marvin.* Elliot was about to confess when Marvin cut in.

In a hostile, defensive tone, Marvin, almost shouting, said, "What? Who the fu...who told you that?"

Both bosses began to speak at once, but Tony gave way to George. "It doesn't matter who told. All that matters is if you did or not."

Marvin began to speak again but was cut off by Tony. Marvin scoffed at Tony's first words. "We cannot tolerate that here. It's a very serious offense and can, and will, result in termination." Elliot knew this was coming, and as much as he didn't want to have to find a new job, he accepted his fate and felt a sense of calm as he fully recovered from his earlier panic.

But, to Elliot's surprise, Marvin raised his voice louder and continued. "What the fuck—"

"Marvin!" George shouted, cutting Marvin off at the profanity, but Marvin persisted.

"What's a 'physical confrontation?' I mean, what the fu...I mean, what does that mean anyway? Physical confrontation!" And with another scoff and a more obvious display of defiance, Marvin went on. "Me and Elliot...we were just playin' around. Ya know, just hittin' around with each other. Everyone does it! If you fire either one of us, you're gonna have t' fire half the line out there!"

Elliot's suspicion was now gone, and he was filled with utter shock. He could not figure out why Marvin would protect him from being fired. Marvin hated Elliot, and this was Marvin's chance to get rid of him. *Was it because he could get in trouble for kneeing me? He could lie about that. The bosses would believe him over me—at least George would. Maybe he just wants to keep me around to have someone to torment. Maybe he wants to keep me around so he can get back at me later. Or...he's just embarrassed he got knocked out by little ol' Elliot.*

Marvin's possible motives kept rushing through Elliot's head. But whatever the reason, he decided that he didn't care. It was beginning to seem like he might get to keep his job.

Tony responded, "You expect us to really believe that? I mean, we all know that you and Elliot don't get along. I've seen you guys myself—you especially, Marvin. I've seen how you treat Elliot. And now you want me—us—to believe you two are just pallin' around?"

There was a pause as Marvin changed his look and attitude from offense to innocence. Before he spoke, Marvin gave an innocent shrug. "Well, you're right. We used t' not get along. I mean, I used t' give Elliot a hard time, but now we're friends."

Realizing that all eyes were now on him, Elliot brought his attention back to the conversation. Tony spoke. "Well, Elliot...are you friends?"

There was a long silence. Elliot was so shocked at the turn of events that he wasn't sure what to say. Finally, he fumbled out, "Uh...yeah."

With a subtle hint of hostility and suspicion, Tony asked Elliot, "You're telling me—*you* are telling *me*—that you are friends with Marvin?"

Again there was a long pause as he looked at each of the men in turn. With an incomplete nod, Elliot said, "Y...yes."

Tony shook his head in disbelief. But he didn't argue the fact. He went on to say, "Well, OK, but you guys did get physical, right? You can't deny that, and that is also a serious offense."

Hostility returning, Marvin said, "What? Are ya serious? No one got hurt. No one complained. I mean, I didn't complain..." He looked at Elliot and seemed to guess that Elliot hadn't complained either. "And Elliot didn't complain. No one got hurt, and no one complained. What's the big fu... what's the big deal?"

With an almost equal hostility, Tony responded, "Horseplay could lead to injury to yourselves or others, or it could lead to damage of company property! And yes, someone complained! Someone brought it to our attention!"

"Oh yeah, company property, God forbid—"

"I find your—" Tony began shouting.

"Guys, guys, guys," George began shouting over Tony and Marvin. Elliot just sat there, still in shock at the drama that was playing out. After everyone went silent, George went on. "Tony, you're right, these guys should not be behaving this way." George glared at Marvin and then Elliot. "*This is not high school,*" he said emphatically. Then, looking back at Tony and ignoring Marvin's scoff, he said, "You're right. They should be punished, but they're a coupla' my better workers. I'd really hate t' lose them. I mean, nobody got hurt, and nothin' got damaged, so..." Unsure how to conclude, George just stopped.

After yet another long pause, Tony spoke. "OK...OK. You guys can thank George, because I don't believe you guys are friends, and I *do* believe you guys were in a confrontation. But because of George here, I'm going to let this one go. I'm going to put a written warning in your records and remind you that two written warnings in a year are grounds for termination. Another incident, and you're outta here."

When the meeting was over, Marvin and Elliot left the two bosses in the conference room. When they got to the bottom of the catwalk steps, Marvin went one direction, and Elliot went another. Neither man looked at nor spoke to each other. It was still fifteen minutes before last break, but Elliot decided not to go back to his spot on the line. He assumed his bosses would stay in the conference room talking for a while, and the person covering his spot wouldn't know he was out of the meeting yet, so Elliot took the opportunity to walk around more. There was so much confusion whirling around in him that he was not sure how to feel or if he even could feel. He was experiencing so many emotions, it was if they were canceling each other out, leaving Elliot feeling numb and indecisive.

Elliot suddenly realized he had wandered over to the boning department, and people were walking away from their posts. He knew it must be break time and decided to go to the main cafeteria, which was near the boning department. The large cafeteria was surprisingly empty, with only a few people spread out at different tables. Most everyone sat alone, with the exception of a couple of people. Elliot walked to the middle of the cafeteria and sat down at one of the many vacant tables. He sat at the edge of the seat and leaned back in his chair with his hands behind his head. Clearing his mind of thoughts, Elliot felt his body stretch, and he focused on taking long, deep breaths, as he had learned during chi-gung training at Shaolin Academy.

A couple of guys sat down at a table near Elliot and started making fun of him, but Elliot didn't notice. He was so focused on the pleasure of his stretching and breathing that he didn't hear his coworkers. But then, something got Elliot's attention. It was a voice, but it wasn't the sound or tone of the voice that got his attention, it was what the voice said.

"Why you guys always talkin' 'bout gay shit? You a coupla faggots, or what?" There was a long pause after Elliot sat up in his chair and looked at the three men, trying to figure out who had said what to whom. There were two men at a table to his right, and Marvin was at a table in front of him and to his left. Marvin was leaning back in his chair with a slight smirk on his face while staring at the two men. The two men were staring back at Marvin with a look of surprise that was turning to hostility.

"Fuck you, Marvin. Since when did you and Elliot become butt buddies? Talk about bein' gay." The men exchanged glances with each other before chuckling and looking back at Marvin.

Without a change in demeanor, Marvin simply replied, "Your mom's more my type than Elliot. And Elliot's more your mom's type, and she told me not t' let you fags get a hold of 'im before she does."

The two men rolled their eyes, shook their heads, got up, and walked out of the cafeteria, mumbling to one another. Without looking at Elliot, Marvin puffed out his cheeks, slowly let the air out, raised his eyebrows, glanced at Elliot, and then got up and walked away. Elliot had no idea what to do or think. He was more shocked now than he had been at the meeting with George and Tony. He couldn't fathom why Marvin was suddenly acting the way he was.

* * *

When Elliot got home from work, there was a message on his answering machine. "Elliot, it's Sifu. Austin told me what happened. I just want to get with you and talk it over. I'll be in the kwoon all day, so you can call or just come in. See you soon."

Elliot was surprised at his sifu's tone. It was not angry or accusing, as he expected; it was neutral, almost pleading. He decided he was just going to go in and talk to his sifu in person. Although Sifu Miller's tone was not accusing, he was sure his sifu would blame him alone for the incident. After the talk and lecture he'd received from his sifu the day before, how could his teacher not blame him? *I know he's going to say I should have had more control; I'm the senior. I can already hear him telling me that I should be setting an example for the juniors.*

The more Elliot thought about it, the angrier he got. This hostility made Elliot eager to go in and tell his sifu that he was wrong and that Joshawn deserved what he got. Without putting any thought into what he was going to say, Elliot was determined not to let his sifu talk him out of how he felt about his actions—completely and utterly satisfied.

Completely oblivious to the uncharacteristic confidence in his step, Elliot entered the kwoon, bowed at all the appropriate places, and headed toward the office in the back of the school. As he approached the office, he did not hear voices, but when he got to the open door and before he could bow, he saw that Joshawn was already there, talking to Sifu Miller. He was so shocked at the unexpected presence that, for a brief moment, his heart and breath stopped, and he felt anger explode in him. For some reason, Elliot felt a sense of betrayal at Joshawn's presence, and he just stared down at the man, who was staring back. Elliot could feel his sifu staring at him also, but he could not take his eyes off of Joshawn.

Quickly, he gained control of his anger. To Elliot, that moment seemed as if it were going to last forever—all three men frozen in an eternal stare-down. It was Sifu Miller who broke the silence. "Guys, let's all relax. Let's sit down and talk this out like gentlemen."

Elliot's eyes stayed focused, and his mind was occupied as he consciously controlled his temper. He was satisfied at having knocked out his larger, more athletic kung fu brother and even felt an unfamiliar emotion: pride. His only regret was that he had blacked out when he did it. He had replayed the incident over and over in his head, trying to remember details, but his memory was cloudy at best. All Elliot could remember was standing over Joshawn and yelling—but not what he had yelled—and then being at home. He did not want to black out like that again. If it came to taking action, he wanted to be conscious of the things he said and did.

Sifu Miller sounded as if he were going to say more. Elliot and Joshawn remained frozen in a battle of stares. And in that moment, before Sifu Miller continued, Joshawn spoke. "Like gentlemen! This mutha' fucka' sucka' punched me! He ain't no gentleman; he a bitch!"

Joshawn twisted his body and postured up a little more, facing Elliot but remained in his seat, as if to suggest that he didn't have to get up for Elliot because he was not a serious enough threat. Elliot could feel control slipping away. His anger almost blinding him, it took every bit of his will to maintain consciousness. He didn't care if he had sucker punched Joshawn or not; he felt no shame for it. In his kung fu training, his sifu and the other instructors were always stressing taking the initiative and using the element of surprise, and that there was no such thing as a fair fight.

Throughout his kung fu training, Elliot, along with the other students, were required to study Sun Tzu. And though he studied the Chinese general intently, Elliot usually had trouble recognizing references to his philosophies in class and answering questions about the text. But every time Elliot replayed knocking out Joshawn in his mind, a quote ran through his head: "One who, fully prepared, awaits the unprepared will be victorious." The other night, Joshawn had been unprepared. And now, in this fleeting moment, he could hear Sun Tzu again: "One who excels at warfare establishes himself in a position where he cannot be defeated while not losing opportunity to defeat the enemy." Elliot was afraid that if Joshawn jumped up, he would not be able to surprise the larger, more experienced man again. And he was not confident that he could take his sidai on equal terms. It was not a flight fear, it was a fight fear—a calculated fear, a warning that was telling him to seek a different advantage.

"Fuck you! '...you shouldn't need me t' 'llow you success. You the tough guy!'" Elliot mocked Joshawn. "Let's take it outside, and there'll be no surprises." And Elliot turned and held his hand out, as if to invite a friend to go first.

Joshawn immediately jumped up out of his seat. Over Sifu Miller shouting, "Guys! Guys!" Joshawn shouted, "Fuck it, let's do it!" and pushed past Elliot, shouldering into the smaller man aggressively. Elliot allowed Joshawn to push past him this way, and when Joshawn had gotten by and had his back to Elliot, Elliot struck Joshawn in the base of the head, once again knocking the large man unconscious.

"Elliot!" Sifu Miller shouted and jumped up from his desk, running to Joshawn, who was lying face down. Elliot just stood there, looking down at his victim. He was in control but still consumed by anger. Crouched down beside his unconscious student, Sifu Miller slowly turned and looked up at Elliot. Elliot could see the look of concern wash away from his teacher's face, leaving that haunting mysterious look. It was the look that Sihing Horvath had had the night before. That look...

seven

Let men decide firmly what they will not do, and they will
be free to do vigorously what they ought to do.
—Mencius

The few days that followed the second Joshawn incident continued to be a blur of intense apathy for Elliot. Elliot had spent his entire life running and hiding from the Joshawns of the world, and when he wasn't running and hiding, he was laying down and taking it. But in a two-day period, Elliot had not only stood up to Joshawn, the very epitome of those who had made his life miserable, he had physically knocked him out—twice. And if that were not enough, in that same two-day span, Elliot had stood up to another Joshawn—Marvin— and had knocked him out as well. These events, along with the mixture of intense new emotions that accompanied them, had pushed Elliot well beyond the brink of shock and confusion, eventually draining him of all emotion and leaving him an empty shell of indecision.

After the second Joshawn incident, Elliot did to not go back to work. It was not so much a decision as indecision. He thought about going to work, and knew that he should, but he didn't really want to. Unable to come to a decisive decision, Elliot just simply did not go back.

Over a few days of aimless thought, Elliot sat in his apartment with the television on, but not watching it, and ignoring phone calls from work and his sifu, but not feeling bad about it. Every once in a while, he would think about finding a new job, but the thought would pass quickly. He knew that eventually he would need to get a new job, but presently, he didn't feel pressed enough to care.

Suddenly, there was a knock at the door. There had been knocks at the door a couple of times over the past few days, but Elliot had ignored them, as he did the phone, assuming it was his sifu. After a few knocks came a muffled voice through the door that echoed into Elliot's apartment. "Elliot, open up! I know you're in there! Where's a guy like you gonna go after quittin' his shitty job? I know ya ain't got no life."

It was Marvin. This sparked a sudden hostility and curiosity. *Why would Marvin come to my house?* Elliot sat up. He noted that while Marvin's comment was insulting, his tone was not hostile—it was joking and almost friendly. There was another knock, and Elliot finally gave in to curiosity, got up, and opened the door.

"Well, well, if it isn't the one-hit wonder."

"What are *you* doing here?"

"I just came by t' see what happened t' ya. Usually, when someone gets knocked out at work, it's the person who got knocked out that doesn't come back, not the one who did the knockin' out."

"Yeah, well, in case you didn't notice, my job sucks, literally and figuratively, and I hate it." Elliot slightly raised one eyebrow and focused his stare a little more intensely on the wiry man before going on to say, "Not to mention, my coworkers were all assholes."

Marvin gave a slight grin and then pushed past Elliot, inviting himself in. Looking around the tiny apartment, Marvin said, "Well, this seems 'bout right for you."

Already suspicious and on guard, Elliot took offense to this statement. Still holding the door open, he responded, "Look, if you're just going to insult me, you can leave."

Marvin turned back to Elliot. "No, no. I'm just fuckin' with ya. No, it's a nice apartment. I've had my share of small apartments." Elliot wasn't sure, but he thought he detected a slightly patronizing tone in the intruder's voice. Again looking slowly around the apartment, Marvin said, "It's clean. I mean, like...girl clean." The inconsiderate man chuckled, turned to Elliot, and slapped him on the shoulder. "Lighten up. I'm just fuckin' with ya." Then he walked farther into the apartment and sat down on the sofa.

Elliot stood at the door for a long moment, staring in at his unexpected guest while still trying to decide if he should have let him in or not, and if he should make him leave. Never having thrown anyone out before, Elliot wasn't even sure how to do so, so he shut the door, went in, and sat down with his guest.

Elliot was very suspicious of Marvin's intentions. Ever since he had struck his former coworker, the man had been acting different...friendly. And it was this that made Elliot so suspicious. Elliot couldn't help but remember a lesson his sifu had given one time: "If you crush a man's ego, he'll either love you for it or hate you for it." Elliot contemplated this lesson in the long silence that ensued. "So, Marvin, what do you want exactly?"

Marvin, who was looking around the simple, plain, tiny living room, trying to avoid Elliot's stare, replied, "Wow, right to it. Uh...I was just thinkin'...I was, uh, I was wrong about ya. I just wanted t' come and tell ya."

There was another long silence. Elliot continued to stare down his guest, who continued avoiding eye contact by looking around the tiny room. Finally, Marvin went on. "Ya know, when I heard ya did karate or tea kwon—"

"Kung fu! It's kung fu." Elliot's hostility began to show a little.

"OK, OK, kung fu. When I heard ya did kung fu, I thought that made ya a bigger loser. I mean, what grade are we in, right?"

Elliot could feel the hostility growing ever greater, but he didn't say anything. Silence made the moment tense, and Marvin could sense Elliot's growing anger as Elliot's eyes continued to burn into him. "Uh, but it turns out ya got some skill. Ya ever do any fightin'?"

Elliot continued to stare, not processing the question. Still unable to hold eye contact with his host and fully aware of the increasing tension, Marvin pressed on. "All the fighters I know do MMA or just street fightin'—fightin' for money. Not really kung fu or that kinda thing." And Marvin started to stutter a little under the weight of Elliot's stare, his loss of confidence showing in his next statement. "I don't know what you're doin' about work, but if ya need cash, I could hook ya up."

Again there was a long silence, and again Elliot was not processing what Marvin was saying. He was too intent on controlling his suspicion and hostility. Then it hit him. Elliot registered what Marvin was suggesting—that he fight for money. The thought of fighting suddenly terrified him, as it had his whole life, and in that moment of terror, he forgot about his recent successful fighting experiences and the anger he was using to intimidate his guest.

"Uh...oh...uh...I don't...that's not really my thing. I, uh...I don't really..." There was a long pause as Elliot struggled to find the words. "That's not really my thing."

Marvin felt suddenly embarrassed for his host as he watched the confident tough guy sitting across from him transform back into the weak, timid Elliot he had worked with and tormented for so long. "It's OK, Elliot. It's OK."

Elliot could sense the patronization in this statement, but it did nothing to rekindle the hostility or stem the fear. Marvin got up to leave, and as he did so, he said, "You think about it. There's money even if ya lose. Take my number and call me if ya change your mind." Marvin pulled out a small piece of crumpled paper torn from an old restaurant receipt. It didn't have a name on it, just a phone number, and he handed it to Elliot.

Elliot said nothing. He just sat there, trying to get control of the fear that now gripped him. He felt frustration at how quickly the fear struck and enveloped him with just the mere thought of fighting. After Marvin left, Elliot lay on his sofa, wrestling with fear and anger. He was afraid of the idea of fighting, and he was angry because he was afraid.

As the conflicting emotions played out, Elliot began to think about what it meant to be a warrior. This was something Elliot thought about a lot and always concluded he did not have what it took. As usual, he thought, *Warriors aren't afraid of anything. They'll fight anyone. Not me. I'm afraid of everyone...I'm afraid of everything.* As these thoughts played over and over in his head, as they had done so many times before, the conflict that was raging in him slowly extinguished, giving way to melancholy.

Elliot went through the usual progression of warrior cultures over and over in his mind, as he often did, until arriving at his favorite, the Spartans. He thought about how brave the Spartans were and how they trained and looked forward their whole lives to a great battle, even, and especially, if it meant death. But what he really liked about the Spartans above all other warrior cultures was their way of weeding out the weak. From birth to adulthood, Spartans were baptized by fire and tempered into the greatest warriors in history. When Elliot thought about the Spartans, he wished he had been raised in a Spartan culture. But today, like every other day, he concluded, *No, I would not have made it as a warrior. I would not have survived the upbringing; I wouldn't have survived childhood. No, I would not even have made it that far. I would have been chucked off the cliff.*

NO! I'm not going to think like that! Elliot suddenly sat up on his sofa and repeated this out loud: "I'm not going to think like that." *I'm no different than any other fighter or warrior out there. None of them had experience before their first fight or battle...or whatever! They all trained, and then they went to battle. And that's what I'm going to do. Fuck it! I'm just going to do it. I can't be the only one who's afraid of their first fight. It's gotta be normal.* Then Elliot thought about something his sifu had said one time about fighting.

In a sparring session, Elliot had been showing obvious frustration at his lack of success. "Everyone has their losses coming to them. A great fighter once said, 'Die a thousand times in your school.' What he meant was that your losses happen right here, fighting your own sipai, your martial arts family. Get your losses here in this kwoon. Die a thousand times right here on this mat, and you'll become a good fighter. You'll already have paid your dues." At the time, Elliot hadn't understood what his sifu was trying to say, but he understood now. *I've already put in my losses. I've been losing my whole life, getting the shit kicked out of me by—*

"Hello, who's this?"

"Marvin?"

"Yeah, who's this?"

"It's Elliot. I just...I was just calling...I thought about it, and...I'll do it."

* * *

Neither Marvin nor Elliot spoke on the car ride. Elliot had spoken to Marvin only a couple of times since he had quit work: once when Marvin had come to his apartment to proposition him to fight and once on the phone. He did not trust Marvin and knew nothing about where they were going, only that Marvin was going to introduce him to some guys who would help him train and get ready for his upcoming fight. They drove for some time on the highway. Then they got off and drove for a few minutes down a busy thoroughfare. Finally, Marvin turned down an almost unnoticeable side street that immediately began to wind this way and that, and they quickly forgot the hustling business district as the street turned into a narrow, secluded road with trees and shrubs growing along the deep ditches. Elliot could see the road winding toward a large industrial building of some sort and pondered the strong smell in the air as they got closer. *I've seen this road in about every horror movie I've ever watched. Where is he taking me? He's probably taking me out here to torture or kill me for hitting him at work.*

Elliot was inhaling deeply again when Marvin interrupted his thoughts. "That's, uh, a potato chip factory up there. They make oil for other foods, too. That's what ya smell."

They need a place that big to make potato chips? Do people eat that many potato chips? Then the road came to a short, steep hill that led to a small one-lane trestle bridge. The bridge was so old that Elliot wondered if it were safe enough to drive on. *I have definitely seen this scene in horror movies. This bridge looks like it needs a "Do Not Cross" or "Condemned" sign on it.* Across the bridge, the road dropped down another short, steep hill and then curved to the right, but they turned left down a gravel drive that turned into dirt and then into tall grass.

Marvin parked by a small, old, run-down, industrial-looking building with broken windows that were boarded up from the inside. Elliot did not notice the building at first because he had been too focused on the bridge they had crossed. The creek that ran under the bridge went straight for about a hundred yards and then curved gently to the right and around behind the old building before trailing off into a wooded area. Elliot could not see the potato chip factory that sat a short distance from them and just across the small creek because of all the trees, brush, and other foliage that grew along the banks. But he could hear the sounds of industry and smell the potato chips cooking.

The small building they were about to enter was overgrown with weeds, trees, and vines, which hid faded graffiti. It made Elliot feel very far from home. Elliot observed that the double steel entry doors looked as if they had been kicked or beaten dozens of times. There were dents, scrapes, and scuffs all over them. Elliot was certain that some of the markings were dried blood.

"What is this place?" Elliot asked as he studied the large slab of cracked and broken concrete in front of the doors. He also noticed the broken remains of walls that bordered the patio-type area and guessed that it was once a large addition to the building. An old brick chimney with a makeshift grill that was obviously still used for cooking caught his eye. He thought it looked out of place, as if someone had built the chimney after the walls were torn down.

"This is Brookwood Hall. Years ago they used t' have punk-rock and metal shows here. Now the Brookwood Fight Club squats here."

Elliot followed Marvin through the double doors, which were propped open by old broken cinder blocks. Coming in out of the blazing summer sun made it hard to see in the dim light that barely illuminated the inside of the old building. The interior was no larger than a basketball court, with two restrooms at the back and a small kitchen area behind a bar near the restrooms. As Elliot's eyes were adjusting to the dim light, he saw that old, faded graffiti covered the interior walls as well. Several guys wearing nothing but training shorts, MMA gloves, and sweat approached. Chris, the largest of the men, shook Marvin's hand and looked Elliot over. Marvin made the introduction. "Well, this is him. Elliot, this is Chris, Jay, Mike, Tommy, and Brazil."

When Elliot got to Brazil and shook his hand, in carefully enunciated English with obvious effort to cover his Portuguese accent, the man said, "My name is Saraiva Carvalho, the third after my grandfather. He was chief strategist of Carnation Revolution." The man smiled broadly and spoke enthusiastically, and Elliot could tell he took great pride in telling people this fact. Elliot was sorry he didn't know what the Carnation Revolution was.

Chris cut in. "You'll hear about his father bein' chief strategist of the Carnation Revolution dozens more times, 'cause he tells everyone he meets. And you can call 'im Saraiva if ya want, but as ya can tell, it's kinda hard t' pronounce, so we all call 'im Brazil."

Still grinning broadly, Saraiva said, "It is where I'm from," with equal pride.

All of the fighters had that look in their eyes, as if they were sizing Elliot up, even Saraiva, with his enormous grin. It wasn't exactly a hostile look, but it wasn't friendly or welcoming, either. Elliot knew the look very well. It was almost identical to the look of Joshawn and every other person who had bullied him in his life.

"All right, Marv, I'll talk t' ya later," said Chris.

Elliot detected a slight tone in Chris's voice and noticed a subtle exchange of looks between Chris and Marvin that seemed a bit off to him. Marvin even acted a bit awkward when he finally turned and left. *Is there some kind of hostility between them? Chris seemed a bit cold to Marvin. Does Chris not like Marvin?* Elliot wondered.

"Well, Elliot, this is Brookwood. We don't have coaches here, or bosses, or anything else. Just each other. We've been fightin' t'gether for a few years now—some of us longer than that—and we'll be glad t' help ya get ready for your fight, but if ya start shit here, then you're out. Got it?" Chris's tone was not hostile, just matter-of-fact. Elliot just nodded and tried to have the same intense look everyone else had. There might not have been coaches or instructors, but it was clear who was in charge.

"Now, we train rough and hard, but we're not tryin' t' kill each other. We'll save that for our opponents. I don't know how much ya know about these fights, but I'm understanding ya don't know much. Marvin tells me ya do traditional martial arts but haven't done any competing."

Although it was not a question, Elliot nodded. "It's all right." Chris paused for a moment before continuing. "Before we get started, I'll go over the rules so ya know why we train so rough. It's not because we're tryin' t' prove somethin' or tryin' t' prove t' each other which one of us is toughest.

These fights are bare knuckle, no holds barred. There are few rules, no refs, and no judges. Anything goes. The fight goes 'til it's finished, so no rounds or breaks.

"Now, when I say there are few rules, I mean very few. First, one on one only. No jumpin' in and helpin' your teammate or any bullshit like that. This isn't a barroom brawl. However, it does happen sometimes, so be prepared. Second, the fight is over only when the loser's team throws in the towel. That means you can beat on somebody 'til their team literally throws in a towel, which brings me to rule number three: only your teammates can pull you off, so if you're poundin' the shit outta somebody, and his team throws in the towel, then only we can stop you. The reason is, when guys from the other team lay hands on the guy who's winning, for some reason, the winner's team flips out and charges in, usually shovin' and swingin'. It always erupts into a big fight with everyone. So, if one of our guys is gettin' beat and we have t' throw in the towel, let the other team pull the guy off."

"Yeah, every once in a while somebody'll get carried away, and when they see their teammate gettin' his face stomped in, he'll run in and grab the guy. It almost always turns into a huge brawl," said Mike, who was tall and lanky compared to everyone else.

"Does that happen a lot?" Elliot asked.

Mike continued, almost uninterrupted by Elliot's question. "Every once in a while, there'll be little scuffles or fights between a couple of crews, and everybody else just stays out of it. But about once every year or so, it seems the whole place erupts into total chaos."

"Yeah," cut in Jay, who Elliot noted was closer to his size. "The last time it happened, the lights got knocked over, and the whole crowd started fighting. It was so dark, ya couldn't tell who was who, but people were screamin' and shoutin' and hittin' and kickin' ya, so ya had to just hit back."

"And after someone started pepper sprayin' the place, ya couldn't see or breathe," Mike cut back in.

Then Chris interrupted the two men and said, "Aside from the multiple broken bones and a couple concussions, three people were stabbed and ended up with pretty serious injuries."

Elliot tried desperately to hide a shudder and was certain Chris had caught it. In his fear that they would see right through him and think he was a fraud, Elliot postured up a little and said, "Fuck it. We're there to fight, aren't we? It doesn't matter to me who or how many."

All of the fighters stared at Elliot with that hard look they walked around with, but now it was a little more pronounced, as if they were trying harder to read Elliot and had not yet concluded what to think of him. Elliot knew they were still sizing him up. Chris had a look that took Elliot a moment to recognize. He was almost certain that it was the look he had seen on his sifu and sihing, but it lasted only a few moments before fading into the same hard look everyone else had.

"Just be prepared for anything," Chris said. After a couple of moments' pause, Chris looked around at everyone and said, "All right, let's get back t' trainin'." Then he looked at Elliot. "Usually we have two groups on the mat sparrin' and one watchin' and coachin'. We really don't have room on the mat for three groups sparrin', so we'll have two odd people out. You and I will be the first odd men out so ya can kinda get a feel for everyone and how we do things here. As you'll soon see here, we don't spend a whole lotta time on different techniques, mostly just sparrin'. You can practice your techniques on your own time. T' us, experience is the best teacher." This last statement echoed through Elliot's memory, as he had heard his sifu say it many times.

Chris left Elliot to go watch one of the groups sparring. Elliot stayed farther back and watched intently at the different fighters while trying to get a feel for and understanding of their styles and techniques. He did not have a martial arts or fighting background outside of his kung fu, but with Sifu Miller and Sihing Horvath's constant comparisons and references to popular fighting styles, he identified with a lot of what he was seeing. In every sparring class at the kung fu school, they would demonstrate kung fu techniques as they applied to different fighting styles and other arts. At the time, it had made very little sense to Elliot. To him, it all looked the same, and even watching the Brookwood Fight Club, it took him a little while to recognize some of the postures and techniques that the different fighters were using.

Mike was tall and lanky and always holding his arms up high and out, throwing a lot of kicks and sweeps. He would also try for the clinch a lot and throw a lot of knees. Elliot recognized the stance and posture mostly as muay thai, a fighting style from Thailand. Saraiva seemed to have the footwork and handwork of a boxer but also good, clean, precise kicks. A couple of other fighters had obvious discipline, structure, and intent in their movements, but Elliot did not recognize their styles or identify them with any particular martial arts. Chris was one of these fighters. He had a way of baiting his opponent, and at critical moments, he would very slightly sidestep and unleash a flurry of devastating combos with precise accuracy. It was a patience game he played: he would attack and then tactically retreat, and no matter how hard his opponents would try to resist the urge to go after him, they inevitably would. It was almost as if Chris knew that the fighters were so prone to attacking that they couldn't help themselves.

Chris had a stance similar to one that Elliot had learned in kung fu, which allowed a fighter to go from one spectrum of combat, like long-range kicking and striking, to another, like grappling, quickly, easily, and efficiently. And Chris kept his hands out a little instead of tight and close to his face like a boxer. This made it hard to find an opening or a weak spot in Chris's structure. Elliot wondered about the young man's background.

It was finally time for Elliot to spar. At first, he was getting shut down and beaten in every way, and he desperately held on to what little confidence he had as each fighter had his way with him. In between rounds, Elliot could feel anxiety overwhelming him, certain that everyone would notice his fear and lack of confidence in addition to his obvious poor skill. He was breathing hard from the physical exertion and the growing anxiety that was taxing him. He also felt exceptionally sensitive to the pain from the beatings he took. Elliot got roughed up a lot during sparring at Shaolin Academy, but never to this degree. This intense awareness of pain demoralized him even further as he struggled to control his fear and anxiety.

Suddenly Elliot noticed the lyrics of the music that was playing in the background: "When the walls close in around you/when all those about you doubt you/when the world can live without you/get a grip, get a grip, and keep it!/You'll see how hard they'll push you/hate your guts and tell you they love you/get a grip, get a grip, get a grip right now!/You'll see how far you'll get pushed/how long they'll hold you down, feed you lies, drive you insane, give you poison to kill your mind!"

Elliot didn't listen to this type of heavy music and was not familiar with it, but the beat and rhythm, along with the lyrics, inspired defiance within him. "Who's this we're listening to?"

Mike answered, "That's Rollins Band, *The End of Silence*."

"I've never heard it."

Then Tommy said, "If ya like it, before ya leave, take it. There's another copy over there. It's great workout and training music."

"OK, yeah, thanks!"

This small token of kindness and friendship boosted Elliot's ego. In his sudden and newfound defiance, Elliot thought of a quote from one of history's greatest samurai, Miyamota Musashi: "Under the sword lifted high, there is hell making you tremble. But go ahead, and you have the land of bliss." This thought rekindled his confidence, and with the adrenaline flowing, he forgot about his fear and pain. The rest of the day wasn't a whole lot more successful, but he started to loosen up a little and relax, which allowed his techniques to flow more easily. The matches weren't complete shutouts, as they had been, and he experienced some success. He noticed that if and when he stayed disciplined with his kung fu, he would sometimes beat his opponent to the punch. Elliot could sometimes even beat Jay to the punch. Jay seemed to have a predominant boxing style with exceptionally quick hands—the quickest out of all of Brookwood—and was extremely light on his feet. Despite how little success Elliot had, it was still more than he had ever experienced in sparring before, and it was very gratifying.

At the end of training, everyone was cooling down and chatting or getting cleaned up while Elliot sat off to the side, contemplating his matches with everyone and their respective styles. He thought about all of the times his sifu had talked about maximum efficiency and how none of the other martial arts had it. Elliot remembered Sifu Miller often saying, "You can take the average person off the street, with no fighting background or training, show 'em the basic jab and cross with maximum efficiency, and let 'em practice for maybe a week, and their striking, at least their jab and cross, will be potentially as effective as an experienced fighter. Show 'em some basic footwork with the concept of maximum efficiency, and maybe a hook and uppercut, let 'em train in those for maybe another week, and they could be at amateur level, easy. Apply those same principles and concepts of maximum efficiency to someone who is already at amateur level, and they could easily be pro. Apply 'em to a pro, and, well, that's just applying our concepts to simple, basic techniques—jab, cross, hook, uppercut—and same with basic kicks—front kicks, side kicks, round kicks.

"Now imagine if you took those principles and laws and understood them and applied them to some of our more sophisticated techniques and footwork. You would be virtually unstoppable. But it doesn't stop there. After you learn maximum efficiency, you'll study the laws of three-dimensional space and the principles and concepts that will teach you how to control that space. And the strategy and tactics that embody the same principles...well, I'm not fool enough to say 'guarantee,' because there are no guarantees in combat. But our kung fu, our martial art, our martial science, will put you so far ahead of all of the other schools and styles that it would take far more than the average or even above average person to stop you. Maybe just your own ego."

*Maybe just your own ego...*Elliot wondered what Sifu Miller meant by that last statement. Then he let his mind wander back to fighting and realized that he was slowly beginning to understand some of the principles and concepts Sifu Miller had taught. The techniques that had confused Elliot so much before were starting to make a little sense to him, and he began to reevaluate all of the matches he'd just had. He first thought about Chris and how he had sidestepped everyone, almost as if he were on a circle, and again remembered his training. Sifu Miller's words echoed in Elliot's head: *"If someone is circling you, then you must attack on the straight line. You must anticipate where he is going to be by which way he is moving and attack their center. If he is coming straight at you, as if he is moving on a straight line, then you must circle, preferably to his weak side if you know which side that is, and attack.*

"You have to circle into striking range and strike! Do not circle and then move in on a line unless you want to go to grappling range! You've just defeated the purpose of striking!"

Elliot imagined himself applying that concept to Chris. He thought about which fighters to use the circle concept on and which ones to use the straight-line concept on. He thought about other techniques and concepts and how they would apply to his new training partners' styles. Mike, holding his hands high in a classic muay thai stance, left his lower body somewhat unguarded. And Saraiva, holding his hands in close to his face like a boxer, left him open to long-range attacks. Some of the other guys who had more unorthodox fighting styles were a little harder to figure out, but Elliot knew that, with a little thought, he could find an appropriate strategy.

Elliot finally realized that nobody had tried for any takedowns or initiated any kind of ground fighting. He approached Tommy and Jay, who were talking together, and asked, "Is there no ground fighting, or does everyone here just not like fighting on the ground?" The two men let out a light chuckle, and Tommy said in a heavy New York accent, "Yeah, anything goes. But these fights are usually done on concrete or asphalt, so nobody wants t' go t' the ground."

Jay added, "Yeah, even if ya take the other person down, ya still get pretty fucked up."

Then Chris, the unofficial coach, spoke as he approached from the bathroom, and the three of them turned to him for his input. "We do a little grappling, but mostly grappling defense," Chris said.

"Do all of the other fighters feel the same way? I mean, does nobody ever take it to the ground?"

"Well," continued Chris, "every once in a while, you'll see a fighter take it t' the ground, but not very often."

Tommy chuckled again. "Usually the two fighters clinch up and stumble and fall."

"If I were you, I wouldn't go t' the ground." Chris gave Elliot a weird look that Elliot interpreted as, "You can go to the ground if you want to, but you would just be stupid to do so."

When Elliot got home that night, he took up his kung fu drills and forms feverishly and with a passion he had never felt with his kung fu, a passion that kept him up all night. He even incorporated the "kiai" that he had learned from Chin Li and shouted it with the release of every technique until Drew summoned the courage to pound on the wall and say, "Come on, Elliot! It's three in the fucking morning!"

But Elliot, with a controlled temper, simply shouted, "Fuck you!" As he went through his drills and forms over and over, he continued to make connections to concepts and principles that he had not understood before. Throughout the night, as he trained vigorously, he planned the strategies and tactics he was going to use against each of the Brookwood Fight

Club members and thought, *Now I know my skills, and I know theirs. Sun Tzu says, "Know yourself and know your enemy, and you will be victorious in every battle."*

Elliot was not able to shut everyone down at the next training like he thought, but, slowly, he was able to apply more and more of his kung fu. He was operating on a conceptual level, while everyone else was operating on a technical level. The others also had particular styles and preferences, whereas Elliot did not, so if he felt that his opponent wanted to stand and strike, he would kick; if his opponent wanted to kick, he would stay in close; if his opponent wanted to clinch, he would stay out and strike, constantly taking his opponents to a range in which they felt uncomfortable.

Though still not completely shutting them down, in a matter of weeks, Elliot was dominating the members of Brookwood, and it made him feel unstoppable. The confidence he gained in those weeks quickly grew out of control, and Elliot didn't resist. Elliot spent long days training with the Brookwood Fight Club and doing kung fu drills from the evenings until the wee hours of morning. He could hardly wait until his first fight, when he could really unleash his power. He wasn't even worried about not knowing the opponent because he felt that the members of Brookwood Fight Club represented such a broad range of styles and strategies that he was prepared for any style of fighter. He felt in his heart that he would finally be a warrior after his first victory.

eight

Violence, even well intentioned, always rebounds upon oneself.
—Lao Tzu

They drove down a long, deserted street in an enormous, nearly vacant industrial park on the lower west side of town. Elliot had never had a reason to go to that part of town, and he was not familiar with it. All of the giant industrial buildings seemed very old and forgotten to him. Some buildings had broken or boarded-up windows and doors that seemed sealed—giving off a tomb-like impression—all behind high, rusty, barbed-wire-topped fences. The empty parking lots were large wastelands of broken asphalt and high weeds growing through the cracks. The streets were in equal disrepair and just as desolate. The weeds looked to be at least thigh high.

With all of the overgrowth and dilapidation, Elliot felt as if the whole industrialized neighborhood was a lost city of some unknown or forgotten civilization. *Where did they go? Was this some Easter Island blue-collar utopia that met with a disastrous fate? Or maybe these are the ruins of some great slave society—some Spartacus revolution where all of the slaves revolted and escaped, leaving the wealthy 1 percent to fend for themselves.* The whole place made Elliot feel cold and empty inside.

Elliot's mind continued to wander and fantasize as they turned onto a narrow street and drove alongside one of the larger vacant structures. He noticed that the street sign read "Paper St.," and he wondered what some of these places used to manufacture. The larger building they were driving next to reached to the edge of the street, with just a narrow sidewalk between the two. Both the building and the sidewalk seemed to span as far as the eye could see in either direction. Then they slowed and began to turn toward the immense structure that blotted out the setting sun, and Elliot saw a narrow opening that let into a narrower drive. The drive was long and flanked on both sides with what Elliot thought was two tall buildings but turned out to be parts of the same building, as the very tight driveway opened up to a large courtyard. There were cars and people everywhere, and everyone gave long looks as Elliot and the Brookwood Fight Club parked and got out of their large, beat-up, puke-green '77 Lincoln.

Elliot realized that what he thought was a grassy yard was, in fact, asphalt that had been nearly consumed by weeds and grass. They walked past the long stares and into another narrow lane that led off the far back corner of the courtyard. This lane was much shorter and darker, as it was even narrower, and the walls on either side reached higher into the sky. The lane ended at very old double doors that were tied open, and beyond was pitch-black darkness. The two very large, rough-looking, tattoo-covered men flanking the large opening barely nodded as the men entered the dark abyss.

It was so dark inside that Elliot couldn't see his hand in front of his face. He looked back to see the fading light of the outside shrinking away and then turned back around to finally see dim light coming through what looked like a slit in a curtain up ahead. This was their only guide, and when they got to the opening and went through, Elliot saw that the curtain was a black plastic that felt like heavy-duty trash bags and spanned from the floor to the very high ceiling and as far as the dim lights revealed in either direction. The lights turned out to be four cheap floodlights on stands all plugged into a power strip and extension cord that trailed off into the darkness. Elliot could not fathom where the electricity was coming from. He saw no signs of power anywhere in the forsaken industrial wasteland, and he heard no sounds of generators.

Elliot looked through the silhouette of people standing around in a large circle just inside the unmarked square formed by the lights and saw the area where it was obvious the fights would take place. The ground was covered with large, dirty pieces of cardboard duct-taped together, forming a large, crude square that spread out beneath the feet of the spectators. Elliot stared at the dirty, worn flooring and, even in the poor light, noticed bloodstains—testaments to brutal struggles and battles between countless unknown warriors. Dried-up pools, splatters, and drips of blood covered the fight area, along with grime and other stains of sweat and puke and God knows what else. As Elliot stared at the intimidating battleground, Marvin hit him on the back of the shoulder unnecessarily hard and said, "At least it's not gravel," and walked on into the anonymity of the crowd.

"All right, you're up," said Chris as he walked up to Elliot from the dark. Elliot pulled off his shirt and felt cool dampness wash over him. Then he pulled off his shoes and felt the grit and grime of the cold concrete floor grip the bottom of his feet. Elliot walked into the light and onto the cardboard, which felt as gritty as the cold concrete. The crowd was mostly quiet, with murmurs and low talking as the other fighter came out of the darkness and made his way through the silhouettes. The fighter was a little bigger than Elliot and much more defined. His hair was shaved close, and he had the same look that all of the other fighters carried around, except more intense. Elliot could see an almost animalistic look of determination glimmering in his opponent's eyes. He was suddenly afraid that he did not have that kind of determination and was even more afraid that his opponent and everyone else could see it. He was glad to be going on right away because he was sure that his courage would falter if he had to endure those looks too long.

Suddenly, Elliot felt a blinding flash of pain as the fighter unleashed a flurry of punches to Elliot's face that made him stumble back. There were no announcements or introductions and no bell or any type of signal to go. Elliot could taste the sweet metallic blood that poured from his nose and split lip. The flurry of punches from his opponent continued to drive forward, just missing because Elliot was stumbling back, almost falling down. As Elliot regained his balance and senses, he instinctively ducked under his opponent's onslaught of punches and wrapped his arms around the fighter's waist. With the same momentum and in the same motion, Elliot picked up his opponent and slammed him to the ground while he remained standing.

Elliot could see the other fighter go ever so slightly limp, and he hesitated in a moment of compassion and confusion. Although all of his previous training was heavy to full contact, if someone was stunned or hurt, you didn't finish or follow-up. That was ingrained into Elliot's body karma, and in that hesitation, the fighter quickly sprung from his back to one foot and one knee and started to reach for Elliot's waist. But Elliot snapped out of his stupor in time to clinch the fighter by the back of the head and knee the man in the face. Elliot was shocked at how much blood splattered from the man's face onto his leg, onto the floor, and into the air as his opponent fell back and to the ground. The blood was warm on Elliot's leg as he again hesitated, watching the stunned fighter grope the air around him like someone who had just woken up in a dark and unfamiliar place. Elliot could see the mob screaming and shouting as they closed in tight around him and his opponent, but he could not hear them. During that moment, while everyone else was lost in their excitement, Elliot was in slow motion, as if in a different world. It didn't even feel like they were yelling and cheering at him. He felt like he was invisible—once again, a ghost in his own life. Then, as his opponent sat up, Elliot kicked him in the side of the head, sending a large splatter of the fighter's blood all over the mob. The fighter collapsed to the ground for good.

Suddenly the sounds of the crowd pounded into Elliot's ears, and Chris, Mike, and Tommy pulled Elliot through the crowd of people and into the dark. The crowd poured around the limp fighter until they obscured him from view, and the globe of light and throng of people began to shrink into the distance. In the shadows of one of the tall floodlights, Elliot could see Marvin arguing with a couple of guys. Marvin had his hands up and was shrugging his shoulders, and one of the guys was poking him in the chest. Then Elliot realized he was being dragged and felt what he thought was warm water being poured onto his chest. "What are you doing?" he asked as he struggled to stand up.

Tommy and Mike stopped dragging Elliot, helped him to his feet, and one of them said, "We thought you were out on your feet." They took Elliot by the arms and helped him forward, deeper into the dark. There was a shadow ahead of him, and he knew it was Chris. As the dark completely enveloped them, Elliot could see another slit of light in the distance. This light was coming from the crack of a slightly opened door. When they got inside, Elliot saw that the dripping on his chest was blood pouring from his face, and he realized that his face hurt. He reached up and felt the blood coming from his nose and upper lip, where a gash in the center of it went almost to his nose. The room was not very big, and in the corner was an old barber chair with duct tape all over it and a card table beside it. There was an older man arranging medical instruments at the table. The scene made Elliot think of espionage movies where people are tortured for information.

The man was clean-cut, with well-trimmed hair and a blue button-up shirt under a plastic apron. They helped Elliot into the chair, and the man turned to him and began roughly washing his face and cleaning his wounds. Elliot's wounds were now a constant throb of immense pain that was intensified every time the man touched his face.

"Well, the nose is definitely broke, but not seriously. It's just a little crooked to the left. I wouldn't worry about straightening it out and risk damaging it further. Not to mention, in this line of work, it'll probably be broken again anyway. The lip, however, is going to require a few stitches. Uh...looks like maybe three or four. So, not too bad."

Elliot began to panic a little as he looked at the table of medical supplies and saw no drugs or syringes. He had scarcely ever been to the doctor or hospital and had never had stitches but was sure they required anesthetics. *Oh God, no anesthetics? Is he really not going to numb me? Oh God, is this guy even a doctor? OK, calm down. I can do this.* And Elliot began to breath heavy as he tried to calm himself, and he wished the other guys would leave so they wouldn't see him show signs of pain or suffering. Finally, Elliot thought to himself, *Fuck it. It's going to hurt no matter what, so I might as well suck it up. I can do this. Pain is suffering; life is suffering.* The Book of the Samurai *says, "A warrior should be careful in all things, and above all, he should not say or think things like, 'How painful.' These are things that should not be said in jest, on a whim, or in one's sleep."*

Elliot tried to focus on his breathing and other chi-gung techniques as the time stretched on and on. The pain was so profound that it made his whole body ache and throb. The throbbing pulsed in a familiar rhythm that made Elliot think of the clock that used to shout out to him every day at the processing plant. It still called out to him in his sleep and haunted his dreams. He looked up, half expecting to see a clock on the wall, but there was nothing but dark shadows encroaching on the small light over the man's work area.

"Well, that's it," said the man as he turned and placed his surgical needle and thread on the table.

"I don't feel so good," Elliot said with a shiver.

"You lost a good amount of blood. Not enough to worry about, though. You're also experiencing a little shock. With the blood loss and shock, I'm surprised you don't feel worse." The man turned to Chris and, just barely loud enough for Elliot to hear, said, "The shock will probably wear off in the next couple hours or so. He took the pain well, and besides his sick feeling, which seems mild, he doesn't show any signs of serious shock. He also doesn't show signs of a concussion, but keep him up for six hours just in case. He can take some ibuprofen for the pain, but plenty of fluids would be better. Some juice or a clear decaffeinated soda would be OK. It will help with the shock. Make sure it's decaffeinated, though. Caffeine is a diuretic and causes the body to lose water, which will make him worse."

"Soda? What the fuck is soda?" Mike asked with a chuckle.

The man, barely turning to Mike, replied without any sign of humor, "Where I come from, it's soda. Pop is something you hear when somebody busts a cap in your ass." This dialog, coming from the clean-cut, otherwise well-spoken man surprised Elliot. The man turned back to Chris. "Other than that, a good night's sleep and he'll be right as rain."

The man turned back to the table as Chris and the others helped Elliot out of the chair. Elliot did not lose consciousness on the way home but barely remembered the trip as he zoned in and out of his thoughts, unsure of how to feel about his victory and the impending scars that would mark his face forever.

* * *

The next day, Elliot awoke to a sick feeling. His body ached, and his head pounded. He had never felt such intense physical pain. Even in his kung fu training, despite the physically demanding workouts and heavy-contact sparring, Elliot had never felt such complete and thorough pain as he did after a couple weeks of training with the Brookwood Fight Club and one no-holds-barred fight. Although his first fight was a victory, his pain and nausea were dragging his morale down. Replaying the fight over and over, Elliot began to question just how successful he had been. *Certainly the other fighter was knocked out*, he thought, but he was unsure of this because his teammates had pulled him away before he had gotten a good look at his opponent. *There was blood. He was definitely on his knees. Did he need stitches also? Is he in as much pain as I'm in? If we're both hurt this bad, did either of us really win?*

Elliot's thoughts wandered to his teammates. He had not watched their fights because he was feeling too sick, but he knew they had all won because each member had been ecstatic about his respective victory. Only a couple of them had slightly bloody noses or lips. *Am I the only one who got hurt? The whole team dominated their fights except me, the one blemish. Maybe my win was just luck. What if the ground wasn't so slippery? If we were on a real mat or ring floor, I probably wouldn't have been able to...*And the idea of luck opened a floodgate to fear as he thought about what could have happened.

Suddenly Elliot jumped up and spoke out loud, "Damn it! What is wrong with me? I'm such a pussy! How can I still be scared? I just...ssst." He clenched his fists, shook his head, and began pacing around his apartment. He took a deep breath and continued his thoughts. *I knocked Joshawn out twice, Marvin once, and I just won a bare-knuckle no-holds-barred fight against someone who trains on a regular basis. I was not lucky! I earned this!*

Then Elliot thought back to his first visit to Brookwood. He was very afraid going into training at Brookwood Hall with new people and even more afraid going into his first fight. But he had convinced himself that the fear was normal and that every new fighter experienced it. He had been able to talk himself through the fear by convincing himself that, after a couple weeks of training and his first fight, he would not be afraid anymore. But, as his thoughts drifted forward to his next fight and then the next and the next, he felt more afraid than he did before. *Damn it! Why am I so afraid?* He walked over to his end table, picked up *Hagakure,* opened to one of the pages he had marked, and read aloud: "If a person is affected by cowardice as a child, it remains a lifetime scar."

Elliot dropped down on his sofa and let out a long sigh as he felt himself sinking into a pit of despair. Then he thought about something his sifu had once told him after he had confessed he was afraid of sparring. "Elliot, fear is a funny thing. A lot of great warriors and fighters have no fear. It was like they were born without it. I don't have as much respect for them. I mean, don't get me wrong, I do respect them, but the person who is afraid, the one who is born with fear and then overcomes it...now that takes hard work and effort... that's kung fu...that's courage."

I am not going to sit here all day. Although the guys from the Brookwood Fight Club all said they were not going to train, Elliot knew they would be there hanging out, as most of them lived there. And he wanted desperately to be around someone—anyone other than himself—because he knew he would think himself into relentless depression if he lay around his apartment alone.

When he got to Brookwood, Chris, Tommy, and Jay were sitting out on the broken patio near the lonely stone chimney. The three men just stared blankly at Elliot as he pulled into the high grass that was their parking area. At first, Elliot thought he might have overstepped his boundaries by coming uninvited, but once he got up to the patio, all of the blank stares turned to welcoming smiles and handshakes.

"Elliot, what up?" Tommy, with his heavy New York accent, was the first to speak.

"Damn, you look fucked up! I guess it's a small price t' pay for victory," Jay said with a slight friendly scoff.

Chris gave a simple, "What's up, Elliot? Congratulations again...your first fight," adding this last bit as if Elliot needed reminded of what he was getting congratulated for.

"Hey guys. Thanks."

Tommy spoke again. "We didn't think we'd see ya for a while. Takin' some shots like that would put somebody outta commission for a while."

This comment didn't sound offensive, nor was it meant to be. To Elliot, it sounded complimentary. "Yeah, you can take some pain. When the doc was stitchin' ya up, ya didn't even flinch," Tommy went on. Elliot felt a sudden sense of pride. When he was being stitched up, he thought for sure everyone could see how weak he was.

Having just browsed through *Hagakure*, Elliot remembered another quote. He thought he could show a sense of humor and demonstrate his knowledge without sounding arrogant by making light of the passage. In a poor Japanese accent, he said, "Ah, *Hagakure* say, 'If one we'e to say what it is to do good, in a single wo'd, it would be to endu'e suffe'ing. Not endu'ing is bad without exception.'"

All the men chuckled. Elliot could tell that Jay and Tommy didn't get the quote, and he assumed they just laughed out of politeness. Although Chris started to chuckle, it was as if he suddenly stopped at the conclusion of Elliot's statement. Elliot noticed this and looked at Chris, who had that peculiar look in his eye. That look...*Did he recognize the quote? Does he know* Hagakure? *Maybe he suspects I'm really a big nerd.*

Before Elliot could think of something else to say, Jay said, "I've never had stitches. I think gettin' some without painkillers and right after gettin' punched in the face...I don't know...maybe I'm a li'l bitch, but I think I'd cry."

Tommy looked at Jay and said, "Yeah, you are a li'l bitch, and I'd definitely make fun of ya." And all the men laughed again. Chris's distinct stare faded away as he did so. Tommy turned back to Elliot, "Man, ya took some serious hits right outta the gate. I thought ya were done for. Man, I can't believe ya survived that. That's a victory in itself."

In jest, Elliot replied, "Well...I *was* waiting for an announcement or someone to say "go" or something—ring a bell. I didn't know someone was going to run out of the crowd and start hitting me. Thanks for warning me." And Elliot chuckled, with the other guys following suit. Elliot felt good and happy. For once in his life, he felt like people were laughing with him and not at him.

nine

The most terrible poverty is loneliness, and the feeling of being unloved.
—Mother Teresa

It had been nearly six months since Elliot had been to the kwoon. Sifu Miller had tried to contact Elliot immediately after the incident with Joshawn, leaving numerous voice mails and even going to Elliot's apartment several times, but Elliot did not respond. At first, Elliot felt betrayed by his sifu. But those feelings grudgingly gave way to shame. Throughout Elliot's life, he was always the victim in confrontations, but he was often equally blamed and punished. He was blamed so much so that he grew to become instinctively sorry and apologetic when altercations and other problems occurred. Even though he kept reminding himself that Joshawn was the cause of it all, staying true to character, he slowly began to feel more responsible.

Sifu Miller did not attempt to contact Elliot as often as he originally did, but he still persisted on an almost a biweekly basis. The truth was, Elliot wanted to talk to his sifu—to answer his calls or go to the kwoon. But when it wasn't his hostility that stopped him, it was his shame.

As he lay on his sofa, swimming in a sea of different and conflicting emotions, he longed for his sifu. He thought about his friends at Brookwood, as he often did, and just as often, it brought him no comfort. He liked the guys he trained with and got along with them exceptionally well, and they seemed to like him just as well, but there was something missing. Their friendships went only as far as training and fighting. Elliot began to realize that they were "work friends." At all of the jobs he'd had, there were a lot of people who were seemingly close friends with each other at work, but he was certain that they barely spoke outside of work. He had even heard people talk about these kinds of relationships. And though he had never had a work friend, he was curious about them. *How can someone become so close to someone else, but when the workday was done, just forget about that person? You clock out of work, you clock out of friendship.* On many occasions, Elliot heard coworkers talk about a close work friend who had gotten terminated or who had quit, and how none of the work friends had talked to the recently departed person, as if contact had also been terminated. It seemed like death to Elliot. Best friends today and forgotten about tomorrow. Those were his friends at Brookwood.

Elliot began thinking about his recent fights in an attempt to boost his morale. He had just had his third fight and, like the previous two, had been very successful. Unlike his first, his second and third fights went off without any injuries, aside from bruised and busted knuckles. And though three fights is not very many by underground-fighting standards, his quick victories and his association with the reputable Brookwood Fight Club were winning him quite a reputation.

That's it! He thought and sat up very quickly. *That's my in with Sifu. Why didn't I think of it before? I'll tell him I was ashamed to come back and thought that if I did some fights I could show him what a warrior I've become—what a warrior he made me. My success is really as much my kung fu training as it is my Brookwood training, maybe even more so. I've won three fights; he'll have to be impressed. Not just any three fights either: three no-holds-barred fights.*

* * *

Elliot was standing in an alley a few doors down and across the street from Shaolin Academy. The afternoon was smoldering, and he could see heat rising from the asphalt of the street, dancing in the ceremony of summer. He looked way up the street, and the heat and haze made the distant buildings and traffic look like mirages. Although he felt sure that Sifu Miller would be proud of him and glad to see him, he was very nervous and wanted to catch his sifu alone. He felt uncomfortable at the thought of other students around, especially Sihing Horvath. This was day two in his stakeout, and the wait finally paid off. Sifu Miller came around the corner from the parking lot, fumbling with his keys as he approached the door. As soon as Sifu Miller pushed his way in, Elliot rushed from his vantage point and shouted for his teacher.

"Sifu! Sifu!"

Sifu Miller paused and stared down the street at Elliot, not because he didn't recognize his student but because he was surprised that Elliot had shown up out of the blue after all this time. He pushed the heavy glass door open as Elliot jogged to a stop. "Elliot, how are you? It's been a long time." Then he gave a bow. Elliot was embarrassed at not remembering to bow first but returned the bow nonetheless.

"Good, Sifu. How are you?"

"Good. Please come in."

Elliot was waiting for Sifu Miller to ask why he hadn't returned his calls sooner, but the teacher didn't. Sifu Miller simply said, "It's good to see you," in a way that made Elliot suspect that his sifu knew he'd come back at some point.

"It's good to see you, Sifu. How are things? How's the kwoon?"

"The same, really. You know how it is. We have a few people sign up, a couple stay, and the rest don't. But what about you? I was beginning to wonder when you'd come in and see us."

And there it was, Elliot's suspicion confirmed. His wise teacher did know that he'd come back. *How? How did Sifu know? Was he just guessing?* Elliot wasn't sure how to feel about his sifu's assumption. Elliot had not planned what he was going to say. He had tried but hadn't been able to think of anything. So he just blurted out exactly what he was thinking. "Actually, Sifu, I felt real bad about what happened and was too ashamed to come back." There was a long pause. "I guess I didn't have the nerve to face you after that."

After a short pause, Sifu Miller spoke. "I was never mad at you, Elliot. I wasn't disappointed or sad. Not at either of you, Joshawn or you. But I was worried about you." There was more silence. Elliot never considered that his sifu would be worried.

Elliot didn't know how to respond, so he just sat there in silence.

Sifu Miller continued. "I was worried because I knew you were having a hard time at work and even in here. Not with Joshawn, per se, but just in general. I knew Joshawn was only making things worse for you, and, in fact, my plan was not to pair you two up or leave you together too long, but I failed to emphasize that to your sihing. All this time I've wanted to tell you that, although your actions weren't OK, I do understand them. It was a mistake, and mistakes are opportunities to learn and grow. You and Joshawn both were at critical points in your character development. Again, I don't want to sound like I condone what happened, but Joshawn needed that to happen. He needed a humbling experience. It just needed to be in a more controlled environment where we could help his ego grow from it. And you needed guidance on developing and controlling your emotions. It's unfortunate that it happened the way it did, but it happened. The opportunity to learn and grow presented itself. Unfortunately, neither one of you were there to take advantage of that opportunity."

Surprised at the things his sifu was saying, Elliot still could not think of anything to say. Of the few scenarios he had imagined, this was not one of them. He had not expected such a positive attitude from his sifu, despite the rebuke in the end. Finally, all he could think was to ask, "What happened to Joshawn?"

"He never came back. It's true that his ego was very big, but it was very fragile. And, as I said, he needed a humbling experience, but his ego could not handle *such* a humbling experience from someone he viewed to be...well...lesser than him. No offense."

Elliot was not offended. He completely understood everything his sifu said about Joshawn and about himself. He could feel that ever-familiar emotion—shame—stir deep within him at the thought of not coming back sooner. He was fast realizing that he had no good reason not to come back. Thinking that he could have been with his sifu all this time made him feel very bad.

Once again, Elliot thought his sifu was ashamed of him, not only for being a bad student but also for being weak and cowardly. It had taken Elliot nearly six months to summon the courage to talk to his sifu. Who wouldn't think he was a coward? Elliot realized that there had been a long silence and that Sifu Miller was looking at him. At first, he began to falter under his sifu's gaze, but he was sure that his sifu would be proud of his accomplishments and that his recent fighting success would wash away any shame that his sifu felt toward him. Elliot just wasn't sure how to tell his sifu, and he was waiting and hoping that his sifu would ask what he had been up to, but Sifu Miller just sat there in silence, staring. Finally, Elliot blurted out, "I quit my job," in an attempt to bait Sifu Miller into the question.

But Sifu Miller simply said, "Really?"

After another long silence, which became even more awkward, Elliot, again beginning to falter, sheepishly confessed, "I've actually been doing fights. No-holds-barred fights." Elliot faltered more and could not hold Sifu Miller's stare as he finished with, "It pays. Not super well but enough to get by...and I've been training."

Sifu Miller's expression did not change. Like a well-seasoned poker player, the teacher casually held his gaze, revealing nothing he was thinking, just waiting for Elliot to confess more. Elliot still could not hold his sifu's gaze. It was not a hard look, and that made it more difficult for Elliot to look him in the eye. He could not tell what his sifu was thinking—if he were mad, glad, proud, or disappointed. Under the pressure of his sifu's stare, Elliot began casually looking around the room, trying to avoid his teacher's eyes, suddenly noticing the heat and humidity in the office. Somewhere in the distance he could hear a fly buzzing, complaining about how miserable its short life was.

Finally, Sifu spoke. "That seems a bit out of character for you."

This statement immediately offended Elliot, and all the fear, shame, sorrow, and awkwardness vanished. With a sudden burst of anger that he tried to conceal, he asked, "Why? Because I'm not good enough? Because I'm not tough enough? Because I'm not brave enough?" Elliot always suspected his sifu thought he was weak and cowardly, but for some reason, when he heard his sifu make a statement suggestive of these qualities, it angered him past the point of self-control. This in itself was a surprise to Elliot, for he had gotten used to his relatively new emotion—anger. As of late, he could manage his anger quite well, but the suddenness with which the anger struck this time made it difficult for him to control.

Before Elliot could go on, Sifu Miller cut him off. "That's not what I mean—"

"What do you mean?" Elliot was still attempting to suppress his rising hostility.

"What I mean is that you seem too smart for that."

"Too smart for what?"

"Unlicensed, unsanctioned fighting. That doesn't seem like you. It just doesn't. I'm not judging, I just…"

Still feeling like his sifu was referring to his skill and courage, Elliot allowed some of his hostility to show. "Oh, so quiet little Elliot can't compete. Everyone else can, but little ol' Elliot can't fight. He might get hurt! Well, I'll have you know I've done good out there! I've won all three of my fights…without fear!" His voice rose slightly, revealing some of his anger.

But Sifu Miller remained calm and simply replied, "I have no doubt you've done well, but that's not what I mean. No, that's not what I mean at all. I just mean that unlicensed, underground, no-holds-barred fighting is illegal and dangerous. And furthermore, there is no honor in it. With your intellect and training, I thought that when you were ready to compete, it would be in a way that would test your skill, not show off your ego."

Lowering his voice but not his hostility, Elliot asked, "How's there no honor in fighting? That's what we train to do. That's what *you* teach! There's a whole wall of trophies and medals out there from your students, and they won them fighting!" As Elliot finished his last statement, he violently thrust his finger in the direction of the trophy case that stood inside the front door of the kwoon.

Sifu Miller paused before replying. His expression still unchanged, he said, "And the legality and the safety?" as if to remind Elliot to address those issues.

Elliot spoke almost before his sifu finished. "I don't care about legality or safety! Who decides what's legal? I didn't agree to the laws! I don't agree to laws or a system that allows rich people to suppress poor people. A system where people are forced to do the most tedious and mundane hard work to barely make ends meet! Slave wages! All while they sit around and get rich off us!" He slammed his fist down on his own knee. "I don't care about laws anymore. I'm never going back to the factory life or blue-collar or any other slave labor." And he sat back in his chair and relaxed his body but not his attitude.

Again there was a pause as Sifu Miller stared at Elliot, remaining calm and expressionless. "OK, what I understand you to be saying is that you've been cheated your whole life; you're not taking it anymore; you believe unsanctioned, no-holds-barred fighting is the answer; and your justification is that it's just competing." And, after another pause, he went on. Elliot began to interrupt, but Sifu Miller held up his hand and began speaking. "Hold on. Let me point out why it's wrong and why there is no honor in it. You're right, one of the main reasons we compete is to test our skills. But it's only right to compete against someone of a similar skill level. In those fights you're doing, no one compares training and experience. You never know if you're fighting someone with more or less experience than you. What happens when you fight someone with little to no training, who may have won some little street altercation or two and thinks they're tough enough for a fight? Nobody tells them no or puts them with another new guy. They get thrown right in with the heavy hitters. What happens when you fight that guy and beat him with all your training and experience? Where's the honor in that?"

Elliot began to speak, to defend himself, but could think of nothing to say, and Sifu Miller continued. "And you *know* the difference between a warrior and fighter." Elliot immediately thought of all the times that his sifu had lectured on the difference and was ready to respond, but Sifu Miller did not give Elliot the opportunity to speak. "Fighters conquer others, and warriors conquer themselves. And what you're doing out there is conquering others."

Elliot could hold back no more and burst out, "How can you say that? You don't know! I'm a stronger person now because of my fights! I overcame my weaknesses and fears. I stood up to those who put me down—things I've never done! How is that not conquering myself?"

"I understand why you think that, but you didn't overcome fear. You gave into other emotions, emotions you've bottled up for a long time—anger and hate. That is how you've overcome your fear, not through courage. Controlling those emotions and *not* giving in to them would be conquering yourself."

Elliot suddenly slammed his fist on his knee again, sat up straighter, and began to shout. But just as quickly, Sifu Miller sat up and, with a harsh tone, cut Elliot off, "You may not have been here for a few months, but I'm still your sifu and still expect respect!"

Some of Elliot's hostility flushed away with a sudden wave of shame for disrespecting his sifu. He calmly sat back down, and Sifu Miller did the same. Then the teacher went on. "Even if you had moments of self-progress or an experience conquering yourself, now what? You cannot move forward without guidance. You need instruction. Those guys you fight and train with, they will never go forward with their character development. And they can't help you with yours. They will always be fighters. If you left and came back in a year, they'd all be the same egotistical thugs just trying to be better than each other, just trying to conquer others. You go back and ask some of them how long they've been doing it, fighting, and you'll be surprised."

"I think you're wrong. I still don't see the difference between what I'm doing and what other fighters are doing when they step into a ring at a competition. Just because it's not sanc—"

"Progression, Elliot. The fighters who compete at amateur, then semi-pro, and then pro are testing their skills. When they become successful at amateur, they move up to semi-pro and then pro. And the pros are always looking for the next great fighter or champion to test their skill against, only fighting the best. Like I said earlier, you're fighting guys who may train but aren't guided in a way that makes them competition for you. It's not fair and—"

Elliot's shame for disrespecting his teacher was fleeting as he lost his temper again and sprang up, almost shouting, "That's bullshit! Those guys I fight are tough, and the guys I train with are tough! You don't know!" He suddenly seemed surprised by his uncontrolled outburst. He had gotten frustrated, even raised his voice to his sifu, in the past, but this outburst was different. He again found himself on the outside, watching himself. Except this time, the Elliot he was watching looked and sounded different.

Sifu Miller did not spring up this time nor raise his voice. He calmly said, "OK, I believe that. I believe they are all tough for amateurs, and I believe some of them might even be at a semi-pro level. But now what? What happens after you beat all of them? Are you going to beat them up again? Are you just going to continue beating up amateurs and newbies? Are you still going to feel good in a year, in five years, beating up nobodies? And what happens when you take a loss from one of these nobodies who doesn't really have any skill and just gets a lucky strike? What happens then? Is your unguided ego going to be able to handle that?"

Elliot just stood there in silence. He didn't know what to say. Deep down he knew the things that his sifu said were true, but he could not accept it. Using his anger, Elliot pushed this realization down deep inside him. Bringing his voice down, Elliot replied, "I think you're wrong, Sifu. I don't think you really know what goes on in the underground fight scene. I don't think you really know how tough the fighters are. You say that professionals are better fighters because it's regulated—well, I think that these fighters are tougher because it's not. They are tougher because there aren't any rules or regulations. You're right about not knowing who you're fighting. Sometimes a newbie or someone with no skill and sometimes someone with great skill and experience, but that's part of the challenge—not knowing your enemy." There was a long silence as the two men stared at each other. Elliot's hostility was slowly subsiding.

Then Elliot went on, his voice more pleading. "You're right about another thing: guidance. It took these fighting experiences for me to put together what you've taught me, and it's made me a good fighter. I've finally found something I'm good at, but I want to be great. With more of your guidance, I could be a great fighter."

Before Elliot could continue, Sifu Miller cut in. "I don't want to train you to be a fighter. I want to train you to be a warrior—"

"Sifu, you can, with your guidance—"

"Not in the underground fight scene."

Elliot could feel his anger coming back. After a short pause, Sifu Miller went on. "Come back to the kwoon. Let's train you for sanctioned competition."

Elliot replied, "Sifu, I like the underground fight scene. I have friends—something I've never had. I make money...I can't...there's no money in sanctioned competition. It costs money. And I cannot go back to a factory. Now I get to fight, I can pay my bills, I have friends..."

"I understand what you're saying. I do. I know things have been hard for you. But I can't be a part of that. I can't condone what I don't believe in."

"OK, you don't have to. I'll just come to classes like usual. You don't have to come to the fights or anything like that. I'll just be like a regular student."

"Elliot, when you, as a student, walk out those doors, you represent me as a sifu. You represent this school and all of the students. Your actions represent the things we teach and do here. As my student, I cannot approve of this lifestyle, even if it is on your own time."

"What do you know about the lifestyle?" Elliot's resurging anger finally got the better of him. "Have you ever been in it? You haven't."

"No, I haven't. But I know plenty of people who have."

Elliot rolled his eyes and said, "Right."

"Elliot, I still consider you my student. I tell you, as your sifu, that the path you are choosing is dangerous and harsh and not as rewarding as it now seems. And it's a choice I don't approve of. It's already made you egotistical and disrespectful to those who love you. If you want to leave all that and come back, then the door is always open, no questions asked. We can come up with alternative solutions to your financial situation. But until then, until you make that decision, I think you should leave."

* * *

Elliot had not been to WabiCha Teahouse in a long time. He had stopped practicing tea and was almost ashamed to show himself out of fear that the tea master, Chin Li, would be disappointed or offended that he wasn't appreciating the gifts bestowed upon him. But the young man was feeling exceptionally lonely after the disappointing talk with his sifu. Elliot had been sure that his sifu would be at least a little proud of him since Elliot's success was a result of his teacher's training. But instead of pride, he felt rejection from his sifu. Now, what little pride Elliot had left seemed to be dwindling rapidly, and he wanted desperately to save it—to maintain it. And though it had been a long time since he had visited his friend Chin Li, and he was not sure what to say, he was desperate for approval. So he headed to the teahouse.

On the way, Elliot wondered what he was going to say or what the tea master would say. *How do I bring up fighting? It will seem weird or too prideful if I just let it out. What if he doesn't ask me what I've been doing these days? It's been so long, will he even want to talk to me? Will he even be there or come out?*

When he got to the teahouse, he approached one of the servers and asked to see the owner. The server was as nice, as always, and told Elliot to wait a moment. A few minutes later, the server returned and bade Elliot to follow her to the secluded back room where the old man was, as usual, sitting alone.

"Ah, it is young Maste' Elliot. It has been long time. Come in, come in. I will se've you tea." Chin Li motioned for Elliot to sit down and then spoke to the server in Chinese. Elliot knew that he told her to bring tea equipage for gung fu tea. As Chin Li was speaking to the server, Elliot sat down at the low table across from the tea master, where he had once sat so long ago. He didn't even have time to greet Chin Li before the old man turned to him and said, "I see you *musha shugyo*."

Elliot recognized the Japanese term for "warrior pilgrimage" and was as shocked as always at the tea master's intuition. *Man, how can he look at me after all this time and immediately know?* "Uh, well, I've...uh, well, I've...I've been...competing."

For some reason, he wasn't sure how to tell Chin Li he had been no-holds-barred fighting. And now, suddenly he didn't want to. The tea master stared back at Elliot, and Elliot could not read the look. It was not a harsh look or a questioning look—or even an accusing look—but it made Elliot feel ashamed.

"You still t'ain w' Sifu Mille'?" as if the intuitive old man already knew the answer.

"Uh..." Elliot did not want to tell Chin Li that he had not been training with Sifu Miller or that his teacher had just rejected him. But, he didn't know what else to say and, feeling like he could not lie under the penetrating stare of the old man, Elliot confessed. "Sifu...he doesn't...he's not into the kind of competing I'm doing, so...so I kinda stepped away... I'm kinda on my own right now. I mean, I have guys I train and work out with, but...as for a teacher, I'm kind of doing this on my own." He said this while avoiding eye contact with the tea master.

Chin Li's look softened a little, and he asked, "You still 'ead *Hagakure*?"

"Uh, yeah, some...a little."

"*Hagakure* say, 'Do not be distu'bed by becoming ronin— *a masterless samu'ai*. If one not ronin at least seven time, he not a t'ue samu'ai.'" Chin Li said this as if Elliot's departure from Sifu Miller and kung fu training had no consequence. It made Elliot feel a little better.

While Elliot was thinking this over, Chin Li's look softened more, and the old man asked, "How is tea p'actice?" This was it; this was the question Elliot was waiting for and dreading most. Before Elliot could speak, the old man said, "You have not been p'acticing." Chin Li's look did not harden, nor did his tone sound critical. But it still made Elliot feel bad—worse than he expected.

"No, I haven't been. I've, uh, been so busy training… for competition…and stuff." Then Elliot had an unstoppable urge to demonstrate his knowledge and ability to quote from *Hagakure* himself, as if to save face. Having just browsed through the book earlier in the day, he was confident he could impress the tea master. "Actually, I decided to give up trying to learn gung fu tea. At least for now. I didn't want it to distract me from my training." With a nervous chuckle, the young man quoted, "'Art brings ruin to the body. A person who practices an art is an artist, not a warrior, and one should have intention of being called a warrior.'"

Chin Li smiled slightly, gave a subtle nod and a long blink, and paused before replying, "Ah, but that only pa't of quote. The 'est say, 'When one has the conviction that even the slightest a'tful ability is ha'mful to a wa'io', all the a'ts become useful to him.'"

Elliot immediately felt embarrassed, defeated at his attempt to impress the old tea master. "The *Book of Leave* also say, 'Original pu'pose of tea ce'emony is to cleanse the six senses.'" And Chin Li's eyes drifted away from focus as if he were in some faraway place in his head, and he continued quoting: "'Fo' the eyes, the'e a'e the hanging sc'olls and flowe' a'angement. Fo' the nose, the'e is incense. Fo' the ea's, the'e is the sound of hot wate'. Fo' the mouth, the'e is the taste of tea. And fo' the hands and feet, the'e is the correctness of fo'm. When the five senses have thus been cleansed, the mind will be pu'ified.'"

The tea master's gaze refocused on Elliot as he went on to finish the quote. "'Do not depa't f'om the tea ce'emony fo' twenty fou' hou's a day.'" Chin Li sighed deeply. "Japan most famous samu'ai unde'stood this concept. He was a'tist, w'ite', and student of tea. He t'avel all ove' Japan and fight ove' sixty duels, neve' lose. He say, 'In one thing, know ten thousand things.' He mean maste' one a't, you masta' all a'ts, Elliot."

Elliot diverted his eyes. He felt ashamed of his lack of discipline and understanding of the other arts and teachings. For a long time, they sat in silence. Elliot tried desperately to avoid Chin Li's eyes while the tea master held his gaze firmly upon the faltering conscience of the young fighter.

The servers brought in the equipage and set up the table while the two men sat in silence. This time Elliot was not feeling excited or euphoric, like the first time Chin Li had served him tea. After several minutes of silence, Chin Li began preparing tea. But the colors of the room did not capture Elliot's eyes, incense did not tease and lure his nose, the kettle did not sing quietly in his ear, nor did the sweet elixir seduce or satisfy him. Elliot noticed that the tea master was watching him intently as he lifted the tiny cup to his lips. "I see you not p'actice way of swo'd either." And Elliot finally recognized the look that the old tea master had been giving him. It was the look he had seen on Chin Li before, as well as on his sifu, his sihing Austin Horvath, and, to a milder degree, his friend Chris.

ten

The visits to his sifu and Chin Li did not have the desired effect Elliot was hoping for. The day following his visits to his teacher and friend, he laid around his apartment, feeling more depressed than he had before his visits. Reluctantly, he got out the tea equipage the old tea master had given him, but it did not bring happiness, as it had the day he brought it home. He remembered back to that first day: studying each piece, setting everything up, and going through the steps and motions of the ceremony without tea because it was too late at night, and he had been afraid the caffeine would keep him up. That first night, like a little child playing tea, he poured imaginary water over everything the way the tea master did, filling the pot with imaginary tea and filling the cups with his newfound euphoria. But he could not get that feeling back. It was dead in him, as was his desire.

After putting away his tea equipage, he retrieved his katana, drew the blade completely out of the scabbard, and studied it with deep concentration. Elliot was not surprised at his wise old friend's observation. He knew that students of the sword had a certain grace in the way they handled things, and he imagined that the wise old teacher could tell by the way he handled his teacup that he had not developed the grace of a student of the sword. Like with the tea equipage, he thought back to when he had first brought the old heirloom home and how happy it had made him. He thought about how he had felt the first night he wielded it—happy, confident. He thought about how he had felt when he wielded it after his conflict with Joshawn and how he had not known what that feeling was, but he knew now—vengeance and hatred and jealously. He thought about wielding it after his first victories in fighting and how he wasn't sure what those emotions were, either, but he knew now—selfish pride. But as he stared, transfixed, upon the magical blade, he felt an emotion he had always known—sadness. The passion was gone, the flame had gone out, and, as with gung fu tea, his desire for the sword was dead as well.

Elliot sheathed the weapon and readied himself for iaido. He drew the blade a few times, shouting the powerful "kiai" every time, but the blade felt clumsy in his hands, almost distant. *"They say a sword chooses its owner."* Yeah, right. *This stupid sword, like everyone else in life, is already ditching me...rejected by a sword. Stupid!*

As depression gripped him tighter, Elliot felt another emotion he was very familiar with—fear. He began to think back to the old Elliot, the weak and cowardly Elliot. Had he really become a great fighter, a warrior, or deep down was he still the sad, frightened young man he had always been? Was his sifu right: did he just cover up his fear with anger and hostility? These questions kept running through his mind, and the fear was growing—consuming him. He began breathing heavy and shuddered. He thought that he had overcome his fear and conquered his depression—destroyed the old Elliot. And another passage he had read from *Hagakure* earlier in the day, a passage he had read so many times before, kept creeping up in the back of his mind, as if to mock him: *"If a person is affected by cowardice as a child, it remains a lifetime scar."*

Elliot sheathed the sword and dropped it to the floor. He pressed his hands to his head and said aloud, "No!" But the phrase kept repeating itself: *"If a person is affected by cowardice as a child, it remains a lifetime scar."*

"No!" And he felt betrayed by his one true refuge in life, the one thing he had always been able to turn to, the one place that was always there: books.

As anxiety overtook him, he wondered if his lack of desire was out of fear. Kung fu, tea, and kendo were all things he knew he could not master, and he began realizing that his lack of desire stemmed from suppressed feelings of fear of failure. He slowly realized that he also had been losing his desire to fight and again wondered, *Am I afraid to fight?* Then he spoke out loud, "I can't be afraid to fight. Look how many fights I've been in. Look at...when I fought...look at Joshawn!" And he slammed his fist into the palm of his hand. But he thought, *Maybe those were all just flukes. Maybe in the heat of rage, I just got lucky. If that's the case, then I'm not a good fighter; I'm just lucky. Oh God, I'm a lucky coward. I've always been a coward.* "If a person is affected by cowardice as a child, it remains a lifetime scar."

Elliot began to replay all of his fights in his head and decided that he had either gotten lucky or had surprised the other person every time. *I surprised Joshawn both times. My first fight, I just got lucky. I surprised him by taking him down. And the other fights...what if there were judges and refs and I couldn't surprise anyone? What if I had to just stand up and fight? My striking is not that good. What if they find out?*

"What if they find out?" Elliot said out loud. "What if... what if..." And Elliot began pacing around the room. "What if I can't be angry? I've relied on anger to get me through. My cowardice...it will show. I won't be able to win...to fight."

He began breathing heavier and heavier. *"If a person is affected by cowardice as a child, it remains a lifetime scar. If a person is affected by cowardice as a child, it remains a lifetime scar."* Then he stopped abruptly. "No! I won't...I can't go back to being a coward. I can't go back to being Elliot." The fear that had nearly ruined him slowly began subsiding as he contemplated. *I need practice. I need to test if I can get angry at will or fight without being angry...*

Elliot dropped down prone onto his sofa, staring at the vast nothingness that seemed to reach beyond the boundaries of his tiny apartment. Suddenly, images of Briseis began flashing through his mind. He tried desperately to not think about her, but the image of her kept skipping over and over like a needle left on a record, scratching ever deeper into his soul. He had been thinking about her more often lately—her straight, light-brown hair that was plain but beautiful; her radiant smile; and her magnificent eyes that would pierce Elliot's chest, stopping his heart and then starting it again with every glance. Those eyes would seem so simple and plain upon a passing glance, but they were deep and beautiful to those who took the time to see them. And he swore that he could almost smell her scent wafting in the air, and it gave him a shudder. His heart sank even lower as he tuned into the music he had playing softly in the other room. It was a song he had listened to over and over whenever he thought about her, and, coincidentally, it was playing now. "Summer dress, your hair's wet, gets into our kisses/Can you tell why my intentions wind up just near misses."

Elliot abruptly sat up and took a long, deep breath. *I need to stop thinking about her.* Then he thought about a scene from one of his favorite movies, *"'Good-bye, my love.' He does not say it. There is no room for softness in Sparta. Only the hard and strong can call themselves Spartans...only the hard...only the strong."* And Elliot imagined he was saying good-bye to Briseis, just as Leonidas did his queen, knowing he was never going to see her again. But that thought did not make Elliot feel any better. On the contrary, it made him feel worse. His sadness suddenly became anger as he began hating himself even more for being so weak. *God, I'm such a pussy. Why can't I just suck it up? I can't think about her anymore. I won't think about her anymore!*

He took out the CD and replaced it with his copy of *The End of Silence*. He listened to the lyrics intently and felt like they were being sung to him. "I think you got a low / self-opinion, man I see you standing all / by / your / self. / un-able to express / the pain of your distress / you withdraw deeper inside." He hated himself more and more as the singer continued. After a while, he was singing along, singing to himself, singing at himself, and hating himself more. "They wrote you off and left you behind!" He got up and started to do punching drills as he sang. "If you could see the you / that I see when I see you." Elliot threw his punches with as much intensity as he could, imagining he was swinging at himself for his weakness. *I'm not going to be a pussy anymore. I'm not going to be like the old me,* he told himself.

Pound...pound...pound...

Before Elliot could answer his door, Marvin's muffled shouts echoed through. "Elliot! Elliot! Come on, I need your help! Elliot!" Marvin's voice sounded different. He was clearly terrified. Elliot rushed to the door and opened it, and Marvin came crashing in as if he were already pushing on the door. Marvin stumbled to the ground and was panting so hard he could barely speak. "They're...they're out there! They're out there!"

Elliot began to panic a little and said, "Who? Who's out there?"

Standing now but hunched over with his hands on his knees and still breathing heavy, Marvin continued. "Three guys...they followed me here. They're tryin' t' jump me. They're sayin' I owe 'em money. But I don't owe 'em nothin'."

"What...what do you mean? Why would they say that? What do they say you owe them money for?"

"They're sayin' I owe 'em money from a fight. But I said, 'I didn't bet you nothin'.' They said they bought my debt from someone." Then Marvin stood up and embraced Elliot pleadingly and continued. "But I don't owe anybody nothin'. They're lyin'."

Elliot walked to his front window that looked out over the street and saw a car creeping slowly by. He recognized the two faces that were looking out. They were the guys he'd seen arguing with Marvin the night of his first fight. They were staring hard at the front of Elliot's apartment building when the car finally stopped. Elliot's uncertainty and mild panic about the situation immediately drained away as anger and hostility surged through his body.

As he turned and stormed past Marvin, he said, "Fuck those guys! Let's go down there!" Without a chance to respond, Marvin quickly followed Elliot like a scared dog being dragged on a leash. Elliot didn't notice. When they got out into the street, three guys where already squared up to Elliot and Marvin. Elliot knew from seeing them around that they were fighters. He had never seen them fight, but he could tell by the way they walked, the way they talked, and their animalistic look of determination, lacking all fear. Their very presence was mean and intimidating, but Elliot had that look and feeling, too. He felt that Marvin and he could take these guys. Finally, after several moments of sizing each other up, Elliot casually opened his arms wide and, with an attitude bordering on arrogance, simply said, "What?"

The guy in the center spoke with an equal tone and manner. "Ask your fuckin' boyfriend there!" Elliot always knew, seeing these men around, that this man was the alpha dog, the man in charge. He immediately began planning his strategy. *I'll kick and grab him first and immediately put him between me and the guy on the right. That will leave Marvin with just the guy on the left. Then I can knock them out one at a time. Even if Marvin is losing by the time I get to him, I'll overcome his opponent while he's not expecting it. Fuck these guys.*

"I ain't askin' him nothin'! I'm askin' you! In fact, I ain't askin' nothin', I'm tellin' you! *Get the fuck outta here!*" The three guys spread out just a little more to flank Elliot and Marvin better, and they inched slightly closer. Elliot could tell by their posture they weren't talking anymore, so he stepped forward in preparation to attack before his opponents did. Then he noticed, in his peripheral vision, Marvin casually backing away. In that moment's hesitation, Elliot felt a hard jolt across his jaw that must have made him black out for a moment. He did not fall down. But in that moment of unconsciousness, the fighter on the right and the one in the center seized his arms, and the third fighter moved in front of him. Elliot felt his whole jaw throb in pain as he tried to bite down. The pain shot all the way up to his temple and back into his ears.

Elliot couldn't see Marvin running away, but his intuition told him he was. One of the men said, "Fuck 'im! Don't worry about 'im." As the third fighter stood in front of Elliot, Elliot tried to struggle and break free, but the other two gripped him too firmly. Elliot could tell these guys had restrained people before. The man in front of Elliot spoke, "Your friend owes us money, and he knows it. He's lucky he runs fast."

"Yeah, bitch-ass cowards always run fast!" Elliot did not pay attention to which one of his restrainers made this comment. The man in front thrust a finger into Elliot's face and continued. "Now we're gonna fuck *you* up," and he looked to their leader holding Elliot's right arm. And the reality of the situation gripped Elliot as hard as the men were holding him. Without diverting his eyes from the fighter in front of him, Elliot could see alpha dog give a slight nod.

* * *

It was dead silent in the middle of the mob that closed in around Elliot; they always closed in tight when it was time to finish, like uncontrollable animals when food was being served. Elliot looked around at the shouting mob, but he heard no sounds. They were begging for him to finish his opponent—begging for blood. The crowd seemed almost tribal as they danced and shouted like participants in a pagan ritual; it was a sacrifice. He made his way through the mob. His opponent, the sacrificial lamb, was on his knees in a daze, unaware of his imminent fate. It was his first opponent, and then the face changed to that of another one of his opponents...and then another and another, and Elliot just stood and watched. The tribe was on the verge of ecstasy in anticipation. But Elliot continued to hesitate, staring at his victim as he morphed. Finally, his opponent's face changed into his own, and he stared down at himself, sitting on his knees, swaying slightly back and forth in confusion. Elliot became embarrassed at himself for looking so foolish. Then he became angry for embarrassing himself. The anger boiled over until he finally kicked himself in the side of the head, feeling the life flee from the body as it fell to the ground.

Elliot woke up on his sofa, feeling pain all over his body. As he came to, he saw his neighbor Drew standing over him. He looked down at his body and saw that his clothes were covered in blood.

"Man, those guys were fucking you up good."

At first, not remembering what happened, Elliot asked, "Wha...what the fuck happened?"

"You and your one friend was about to get into a fight with these three guys. Then your friend ran off. After that, the three of 'em, they jumped you. They looked pretty mean, and I was by myself, so I yelled out to 'em that I called the cops. They told me to mind my own fuckin' business, but they left anyways."

Elliot began to remember what had transpired as he attempted to sit up but fell back in pain. As he regained more and more of his senses, he noticed that more areas of his body hurt, and the pain began to intensify. He clutched his sides as he realized how much it hurt to breathe or move any part of his body.

"Your ribs look pretty bad. I can't tell if any are broken. They were puttin' a good stompin' on you."

Elliot also noticed that his limbs hurt. The pain was so intense that he thought all of his bones were broken. He looked at the back of his left hand and saw a shoe print across his fingers. Then he noticed shoe prints on his arms and his dirty, blood-soaked shirt and jeans. He imagined them kicking and stomping on him while he was down. He reached up and felt his bloody face. His nose was bleeding and hurt like it did the night of his first fight. *Great, broken again. That doctor or whatever was right.* Then he felt that his lip was bleeding from a couple of places and that his upper front teeth hurt. They didn't feel loose, but it hurt to apply even the slightest pressure on them. On the right side of his forehead, he felt a large lump with a gash on it. The blood felt dirty and gritty, and when he looked at his hand that touched the gash, he saw dirt and small fragments of asphalt from where his head had either hit the ground or had been stomped into the street. He ran his hand over his head and found a combination of dry, crusty blood and wet, fresh blood in his hair around similar lumps. *God, how many times did they stomp on me?*

"Man, are you gonna be all right?"

Elliot groaned as he tried to adjust to a more comfortable position and then said, "I need you to do me a favor. I need you to call someone for me."

He had Drew call Chris and tell him what had happened. Elliot listened as he heard Drew telling what little he'd witnessed and knew that the lack of information would only drive Chris's curiosity harder. Elliot suspected Chris would show up very soon, and, indeed, it seemed like no time had passed before there was a knock at the door. After Drew let Chris and Tommy in, he told Elliot, "If you need anything, just give me a shout." As the neighbor started to turn and leave, he caught sight of the sword hole that now linked their two apartments and smiled. "You can shout through there." Too anxious to hear about what happened, Chris and Tommy ignored the mysterious hole in the wall and waited for Drew to leave.

"Man, you look like shit! What the fuck happened?" Chris asked as he knelt down beside the sofa and immediately began helping Elliot sit up. Elliot spent the next few minutes recounting exactly what had happened without interruption from the other two. During his narrative, he noticed Chris and Tommy exchange looks a couple of times. When Elliot finished, the other two were looking down at the floor in contemplation.

A few moments went by before Tommy broke the silence with his heavy New York accent that seemed to sound heavier than usual. "Well, Marvin's a piece a shit. It doesn't surprise us at all. At least...it doesn't surprise me."

"Me either," said Chris. "Marvin's a fucker, and we don't really even like him."

Before Chris could say more, Elliot interrupted. "Then why do you guys hang out with him?"

"Well, we don't hang out with 'im. We only know 'im from the fight scene. He's kinda an unofficial fight promoter. He introduced a couple of us to the fight scene, and he some-times arranges fights. His problem is, he gambles away the money he makes from the fights on the fighters. That's why he works where ya used to work, cleaning up turkey shit or guts or whatever." Before Chris went on, he looked at Tommy and said, "Go call Hyde."

"Who's Hyde?" asked Elliot, now resting back on his sofa.

As Tommy took the phone into the other room, Chris answered Elliot. "He's the guy who stitched you up at your first fight."

Losing a little bit of composure and allowing a little panic to show, Elliot opened his eyes wide and said, "Oh God, is that guy even a doctor?"

"Well, he used t' be. He lost his license or certificate or whatever doctors need a long time ago in a malpractice suit. After his career fell apart, his wife took their kids and left. She took 'im for everything he had. After that, so the story goes, he turned t' the only other thing he knew how t' do: fight. Turns out he wrestled in high school and college and did some golden-glove boxing or some shit. He's old-school—a generation or so ahead of us on the scene. He went undefeated for years. It's hard tellin' what his record is. He never talks about it, and it seems t' get more exaggerated as time goes on. Back in the day, when he was still fightin', if someone got hurt bad, he would always jump in and help 'im. Sorta like a first responder kinda thing. He even started stitchin' and stuff like that. The old-schoolers say that, on more than one occasion, he'd bust somebody up and then stitch 'im up afterwards."

Upon reentering the room, Tommy interrupted. "I heard one time he gave himself stitches." And after a pause, as if lost in thought, he said with a slight chuckle, "Like fuckin' Rambo style."

When Tommy finished, Chris cut back in. "He got to where he was bandaging fighters up so much, he didn't have time t' fight himself. Because he was a doctor and a fighter, people started callin' 'im Dr. Jekyll and Mr. Hyde. That was sorta his fight name. After a while, everyone musta realized what a lame-ass name it was, and people just started callin' 'im Dr. Hyde. Even that name is kinda lame, so most people on the scene nowadays just calls 'im Doc or Hyde."

After Chris finished, the three of them sat in silence. Elliot was having a hard time breathing because of his broken ribs and was trying desperately to ignore the pain of his battered limbs and pounding head. Finally, in an attempt to distract himself from the pain, and out of sheer curiosity, he asked, "Do you guys know the three who jumped me?"

Chris answered, "Yeah, those three and a couple more think they're some kinda underground, organized-crime syndicate or some shit like that."

Tommy cut in with, "Really, they're just a buncha wiggers."

There was a long pause as Chris and Tommy both looked down at the floor. Elliot could feel they were struggling with something. Finally, Chris looked back at Elliot. "Look, there's somethin' we have t' tell ya." He exchanged looks with Tommy before continuing. Elliot saw the look and detected a note of unease in Chris's voice. Speaking quickly, Chris said, "Marvin has been bettin' against you, and we knew it. When he first brought ya to us, he said ya had some kinda cheesy martial arts background and ya thought you could fight. He said really ya were a little bitch crybaby. He said he convinced ya t' do a fight but knew you were too much of a pussy t' do anything. He told us he needed us to train with ya enough t' make ya feel comfortable enough t' fight. He just wanted to get ya t' do at least one fight. He said it'd be easy money for 'im and was sure you'd lose. After ya won your first fight, he was sure he could win 'is money back on your second fight. He thought your first win was a fluke. But ya kept winning. I told 'im we wouldn't fake or pretend like you were tougher than any of us. I said we weren't going t' trick ya. We would spar with ya, and if ya lasted with us, then ya did, if ya didn't...well, ya didn't."

"So..." But that was all Elliot could get out. He didn't know what to say and was immediately offended. Deep down, he was hurt because he liked all of the Brookwood Fight Club, and he thought they were sincere in liking him. But now he felt betrayed.

"Ya just kept winning, and Marvin kept losin' money on ya, thinkin' your wins were luck. He really thought ya didn't have it in ya. He kept bettin' double or nothin'. And now he can't pay, and those assholes are tryin' t' take it outta his ass."

Elliot could barely concentrate on the story Chris was telling. He thought back to his first day of training with the Brookwood Fight Club and remembered how he thought they all looked like tough-guy assholes and expected more of a Joshawn attitude from them. The day he met them, for a brief moment, he felt suspicious at how welcoming they were and at how tolerable they were when he was getting beaten so easily and so often. Now it was obvious—they hadn't wanted him to fail or quit. *Why would they do that? If they hate Marvin so much...why? You can't count on nobody.*

Elliot wanted to scream and shout at them. When he had first met them, it took him a while to like them. All along, he was afraid that they were like everyone else—selfish, mean, arrogant. But they seemed sincere, so Elliot let his guard down and began to open up and become friends with them. He couldn't speak, because he feared his anger would give way to sorrow. He had felt like these guys were the first real friends he'd ever had, and it turned out they were part of a plot to humiliate and hurt him. *Just like everyone else.*

Chris went on. "Look, I'm sorry." Then he exchanged looks with Tommy. "*We're* sorry. At first we thought you *were* kinda a little bitch. You seemed weak, and ya couldn't fight very good. We figured after the first week you'd quit, and that would be the end of it. But ya stayed in there, and that kinda determination means a lot t' us. And as we got t' know ya, we all started likin' ya. You just kinda started workin' out, so we figured why tell ya? Whether ya won or lost your first fight didn't matter; we wanted ya t' keep trainin' with us."

There was another long silence as Elliot continued to stew. After a while, Chris sighed and spoke again, with a resigned air. "If ya don't want t' train with us anymore, that's cool. I'd probably hate us, too. We'll wait for Hyde, and after he fixes ya up, we'll go. If you wanna talk t' us or even train, then ya know where we are. You're always welcome."

Elliot held his eyes closed and leaned his head back on the arm of the sofa as he used his chi-gung training to calm his emotions. He wanted so badly to believe Chris, to convince himself that Chris sounded sincere and that, in all actuality, they really hadn't done anything wrong. It was all Marvin. *Marvin!* He realized he was not used to having friends, and he tried to tell himself that friends make mistakes and they also forgive each other. *These guys are the only friends I have. I guess they've never given me any other reason to distrust them.*

Still suspicious, Elliot said with a sigh, "No, you guys can stay. I mean, I'd like it if you guys hung out." And though he believed he would not have done the same thing, he said,

"I would have done the same thing. You guys didn't know. Well, you did know, but I still don't blame you." To Elliot, the long silence that ensued indicated their understanding that he had forgiven them. He knew it had been a struggle for them to apologize.

Finally, Tommy broke the silence in an excited hostility that made it clear that what was done between them was now resolved and forgotten. "I say we go fuck Marvin up!" Chris nodded, but his eyes stayed fixed on the floor. He hadn't quite finished feeling bad. Elliot said nothing but was in agreement with Tommy. But Elliot wanted more. He felt that a beating would not be enough. He wanted Marvin to feel the sense of panic that comes when a person watches his friends abandon him, realizing they weren't his friends after all. Elliot began to form a plan in the silence that once again enveloped the room.

Again it was Tommy who broke the silence. "I say we go right now. You know 'is bitch ass ran home. I say we go over there, knock on the door, and drag 'is ass outside."

Elliot noticed Tommy's accent thickening as the young man got more and more excited at the prospects of kicking Marvin's ass. But deep down, Elliot knew it wasn't just kicking Marvin's ass that excited Tommy. It was the prospect of kicking anyone's ass—the prospect of fighting, period. He didn't even have to look up to know the look Tommy had; he could sense it. Like all fighters locking in on a target, Tommy was like a wild animal that had just caught scent or sight of its prey and was now eager for its meal to come.

"I have a better idea," said Elliot. Chris finally looked up as the last feelings of guilt fled from him. With both of the men's full attention, Elliot opened his eyes, looked at them, and continued. "This is what we do: first, we tell Marvin that I'm not mad at him." Chris and Tommy both started to protest, but Elliot stopped them. "Just wait…listen…we tell Marvin I'm not mad. We convince him. We tell him we, as in the Brookwood Crew, want to fuck those other guys up, but they won't meet us anywhere because they don't want trouble, they just wanna get paid. We'll tell Marvin that one of their guys wants to fight him even-up for what he owes them. That is, if Marvin wins, his debt is clear. If he loses, he still owes them, and we, the Brookwood Fight Club, pay. We tell Marvin they think we're still mad at him, and as punishment for leaving me hanging, we're going to let them jump him. Then we tell Marvin it's a trick and that right when they're about to jump him, we all jump in and fuck their whole crew up. Marvin thinks it's just a trick to lure those pussies out and meet us somewhere."

"But what about Marvin? Are we goin'a fuck him up too?" asked Tommy in a panic, fearful they were going to let Marvin off the hook.

"Ah, that's the best part. We go to those other guys and convince them I'm—we're—not pissed at them because they did the right thing and that we would have done the same thing. We explain to them that Marvin lied to me and then left me hanging, which they witnessed. We tell them we have no beef with them and that it's Marvin we want justice from. We tell them we talked Marvin into agreeing to fight just one of them for the debt he owes. The good part is, we tell them that right when Marvin and whoever is about to throw down, they can all jump Marvin while we just watch. They think this is all a trick to lure Marvin out. They get what they wanted in the first place, to beat down Marvin, and I get revenge on Marvin for getting jumped on his account.

"Then, after they lynch Marvin for a few minutes, and while they're not paying attention, we jump them. That way, Marvin gets what he has coming from them *and* me, and *they* get what they have coming from me, and everyone is satisfied. They get justice on Marvin, and we get justice on Marvin *and* them. All in one fell swoop."

Once again, Tommy was the one who broke the long silence that followed as they took in Elliot's elaborate plan. "Jesus, that's pretty fuckin' hard-core. I like it."

Then Elliot noticed that look on Chris's face again as Chris's eyes burned into him—the same look he occasionally saw on his sifu's, Austin's, and even Chin Li's face, and now Chris's. As always, he couldn't put his finger on what the look meant or what any of them were thinking when they had that look. "That's pretty fuckin' devious. It turns out you're not just a good fighter but quite the strategist also."

With that look and the ambiguous tone in Chris's voice, Elliot couldn't tell if his statement was a compliment or not. He just slowly lay his head back down on the armrest, closed his eyes, and said, "Sun Tzu says, 'The way of victory is deceit.'"

The three men spoke very little as they awaited Hyde. Elliot lay in nervous anticipation, certain he would be stitched up again, even more this time. It was not a long wait for the infamous doctor to arrive. "Yeah, they busted you up good. It looks like I'm going to have to stitch that lip again. There's a couple spots on your head. We can wrap your ribs, but there's not much more to do about that. All in all, they don't look *too* bad. Your hand and fingers look broken. I can't tell for sure without an X-ray, but I'm pretty sure. If so, probably more displaced than non-displaced fractures. Personally, I recommend seeking a medical professional. I don't have the necessary resources to reset bones if they heal wrong."

Although the thought of not getting professional medical attention scared him, Elliot knew he could not and said, "I don't have insurance or very much money."

"You guys don't offer health insurance?" and the man turned slightly to Chris and Tommy. Although the statement seemed to be made in jest, the man had no look of humor on his face.

"Even if we did, these injuries didn't happ'n on our clock. Shit!" Tommy blurted out with a scoff.

Hyde had turned back to Elliot. "I don't have material to make a real cast, but I do have stuff to wrap it as good as a real cast. You're just going to have to be extra careful with it and pray they heal up OK. It will take a few weeks for the bones to heal enough to take the wrap off. And then you won't be able to hit anything for a few weeks after that.

Most everything else *seems* OK. All your limbs and joints are pretty banged up but don't seem broken—just bruised and swollen. If the swelling in these areas doesn't go down in a few days or if anything gets worse, you'll have to call me."

The pain from Hyde poking, prodding, and moving Elliot's limbs around was excruciating, and Elliot thought for sure he was going to either throw up or pass out. When the man was done examining him, Elliot relaxed back on his sofa and closed his eyes again, struggling to control his anxiety. He began to think that his tolerance to the pain the first time he was stitched up was due to being stunned and the adrenaline that was flowing through him from the fight. But this time, he was painfully lucid, and there was no adrenaline. There were just his own thoughts, telling him that he was weak and that his friends were sure to see it this time.

As Hyde was getting his tools ready, he spoke to Elliot. "Chris mentioned before that you train with Sifu Miller."

Elliot was surprised at this statement. Chris and some of the other guys at Brookwood had asked about his training one day, and Elliot had mentioned as casually as he could that he trained under Sifu Miller. But it was such a quick passing statement, and none of the members of Brookwood had asked any more questions on the topic. He was sure no one cared to remember, which was what he was hoping. Elliot learned very early on that there is not a lot of respect for traditional arts in the underground fight scene, so he was careful not to mention his background any more than he had to. And he assumed that's why the subject was pursued no further. The fact that Chris had been talking to others about his background made him nervous. "Uh...yeah...I trained under him for a while." Being afraid of what the doctor might think of him and his traditional background, Elliot started to make an excuse for training under Sifu Miller. "I, uh, heard he trains people to fight, but...uh, I found out quickly they don't do that there at that school. So I left."

"Really?" The man stopped setting out his equipment and turned to Elliot. And with an air of surprise, he said,

"I've always known Sifu Miller to turn out great fighters. I mean, those who actually stay with it and become serious students...they always turn out to be great fighters." Then the doctor turned back to his equipage. "I mean, you never see 'em on the fight scene, but if you go to sanctioned competitions, those guys usually dominate."

Elliot felt embarrassed and surprised. He was embarrassed because he felt he had just been caught in a lie. He was surprised because, in the time he had trained under Sifu Miller, none of the serious students had entered any competitions. And he was surprised that Hyde knew his sifu. Then the doctor asked a question that surprised Elliot further: "Does Austin Horvath still train under Sifu Miller?"

Elliot was so surprised that he didn't respond right away. It was not until the doctor again stopped his preparation, turned, and stared at the battered young man that Elliot responded. "Uh, yeah...yeah, he still trains there." The doctor turned back to his tools, and, after a short pause, Elliot asked, "How do you know them?"

"Well, I only know Sifu Miller by reputation. I know Austin from back in the day. He was fighting when I was still fighting."

The surprise being too much, Elliot abruptly sat up, ignoring his pain, and asked, "You mean fight, as in, on the scene?"

"Oh, yeah." Hyde stopped what he was doing and looked up and into the distance, as if he were looking way back in time. "He turned out to be a great fighter. He was coming up as I was getting out of fighting, so we never fought each other." The doctor turned back to finalize his preparations.

Elliot felt a sudden hostility brewing in him. He had just asked his sifu if he would train him to fight, and Sifu Miller had refused. *Had he trained Austin? How could he have trained Austin and not me? He acted so righteous. Did he train Austin?* "Was Austin with Sifu Miller at the time?"

Hyde turned to Elliot with a white towel and a bottle of liquid in his hands. "Oh, no. No, he was with this karate sensei guy...Sensei...Sensei Ushigei. Sorry 'bout that. It took me a minute to remember his name."

Hostility turning to deep curiosity, Elliot asked, "What... what happened? I mean, why'd he leave Sensei Ushi...Ushi... Ushigei or whatever?"

The doctor moved close to Elliot in a way that made Elliot feel awkward, so he lay back on the sofa. The doctor put his hands on the sofa, holding the towel and bottle beside Elliot as if to rest on them, and in a more serious tone replied, "I never got to fight Austin, but I did get acquainted with him. He came from a long line of military men. His whole family was military, Marines mostly, including him. But his military career was short. For some reason, he was dishonorably discharged. I never knew him well enough to ask why, nor did anyone really know. There was only speculation. After the military, he got into fighting. At first he was OK—some wins, some losses. Then he hooked up with Sensei Ushigei, and he became very, well, he didn't lose any more. Even before Sensei Ushigei, Austin was very violent and, well, Sensei Ushigei encouraged that from his students. I don't know if Austin was violent because he got kicked out of the Marines, or if that's what got him kicked out, or what, I just know that he was not to be trifled with. And when he got with Sensei Ushigei, he became worse.

"One of the other things that Ushigei made his students do was go around and challenge other martial arts teachers in the area. Every time a new martial arts school opened up, he'd send in his top student to challenge the teacher, and, well, his students always won. Usually, out of shame, a defeated teacher would close his school, or most of his students would quit, and some of them would join up with Sensei Ushigei. Back in the day, there weren't any traditional martial arts schools around here because Sensei Ushigei would extort money or run them off. If the defeated teachers or masters wouldn't pay or close their school after being defeated, Sensei Ushigei and his students would resort to terror and vandalism.

"In fact, Austin and Sensei Ushigei and some of his other students got into a lot of trouble over arson, or maybe it was attempted arson or something like that. I heard Sensei Ushigei was going to get into a lot of trouble because he was the ringleader, and there are some kind of laws nowadays that target ringleaders of organized crime. I think the law is called 'Rico' or something like that. It was not Ushigei's first offense. Supposedly, the D.A. had been building a case against him for years. Everyone assumed that Sensei Ushigei fled back to Japan, where he's from. Austin never got in any other trouble that I know of, but for a short time he continued fighting and going around challenging martial arts teachers when a school opened. That is, until he met Sifu Miller. Now I heard that he went in and challenged Sifu Miller and got his, well, got his ass handed to him. And, as if that were not enough, Austin went back and tried again and got his ass handed to him a second time. After that, Austin became Sifu Miller's student."

Hyde sat back up and began wetting the towel with liquid from the bottle. Elliot was so shocked at the fascinating story about Austin that he didn't have anything else to ask. As the man thoroughly wiped Elliot down and then began suturing him, Elliot lay there, thinking about his sihing and his sifu. He forgot about his aching body while his mind wandered and dreamed of having such a reputation, all while the needle penetrated and the thread pulled. Several minutes went by, and Elliot was so deep in thought that he didn't notice who asked, but one of the other two men asked the doctor why he quit fighting.

Without stopping or breaking his intense concentration, the doctor responded in a slow calculated voice. "Well, gentlemen, the underground fight scene is a dead end." Elliot noticed both of the other men scrunch up their faces in silent scoffs, but it didn't stop the doctor. "You can't go on to be a professional fighter from here. To get a pro fight, you have to have a record, and unlicensed fights don't count. In fact, the way the business is now, if a manager or promoter or anyone from the State Athletic Department suspects a fighter of doing unlicensed fights, they won't have anything to do with him. Not to mention potentially getting banned from any and all sanctioned competitive fighting. That means you have to have an amateur record, and you don't make money fighting amateur. It actually costs money to compete in amateur fights." After a short pause, the man went on. "So you can't quit your day job. Even after you start in the pros or semi-pros, the payout is so little that you need a secondary income. Unlike the underground scene, the people you train with—the gyms and clubs and schools—they all cost money. I imagine it's difficult to keep up with the pros who can afford to train all day while you're at work. And since you can't go pro from the fight scene, you can only keep fighting unlicensed fights, and though they can sometimes pay pretty decent, you'll never get paid more. A few fights a year making a few hundred dollars, maybe a grand a fight, doesn't add up to much at the end of the year. And you're certainly not going to get any sponsors on the scene."

"I've seen fights pay in the thousands," Tommy interrupted in protest.

The older man paused in the middle of a suture. "Yeah, but how often? I mean, I know every once in a great while there'll be a big payout, but not very often. Even if you made a couple grand for one fight this year, the rest of the few fights you do will only be in the hundreds. Unless you're squatting somewhere or living with your parents, you can't live off that."

Elliot could sense the denial and frustration radiating from Chris and Tommy, who didn't want to hear or believe the old fighter. Elliot didn't want to believe him, either. Elliot had recently, deep down, began to question the long-term future and prospects of what he was doing. And the recent conversation he had had with his sifu, along with Hyde's statements, compounded the uncertainty of his future.

"And the monetary aspect's not even the worst part. The worst part is that the competition never gets better. Most of the time you're fighting some two-bit bar stalker with no real training. And the other times you might fight someone with some mixed training and a little fighting experience, but all the serious fighters are in legal, licensed circuits."

Tommy, now losing his temper, shouted, "What the fuck are you talking about? We all train real hard. You're right, we might not be livin' a rock-star lifestyle, but we don't give a fuck about that! We're warriors! We're soldiers!"

Without any signs of perplexity, Hyde simply replied, all the while suturing Elliot, "You guys are the exception. I know you guys, and I know you train hard and serious. But not all the guys you fight do the same. You guys are fighting punk-ass amateurs. You're the guys who should be fighting entry-level pro or semi-pro fights, but instead you're beating the shit outta the same nobodies every week. What the fuck does that prove?" Despite his distracting pain, Elliot noticed the doctor break character. And though the older man's tone was not harsh, his words were, and for a brief moment, Elliot could imagine this man of seeming propriety kicking the shit out of someone.

Tommy jumped up and stomped at the man as if he were trying to frighten away a barking dog. "Man, who the fuck are you? Who the fuck are you to judge me? You don't know me! Man, fuck you!" And the angry young fighter stormed out of the apartment. Chris made not a sound or movement; he just sat there, listening intently and watching. The doctor didn't flinch or miss a beat at the young man's outburst, as if it hadn't even happened. Elliot continued to contemplate everything the man said and was hit with a sense of déjà vu, as he had heard his sifu say the same thing the day before. He lay very still, tolerating the pain of the doctor's hands but suffering from the truth of his words.

eleven

After driving down narrow roads in the midst of sea upon sea of cornfields, visible in the moonlight, their caravan turned down a long, overgrown gravel lane. At the end of the lane was a clearing, and in the center was an old boarded-up little building that had started to crumble. They parked their cars near the building, facing their headlights toward the lane. Elliot got out and stared up at the night sky. He realized he had never seen the stars so clearly. He couldn't remember the last time he'd left the city; if he'd ever left the city. He slowly and reluctantly admitted to himself that it was not lack of reason but a general fear that had kept him there. Though he had always wanted to travel and visit other places, the thought had always made him nervous.

They had driven for nearly an hour, well beyond the light pollution of the city. It was as if he were seeing stars for the first time. Someone bumped into him as everyone climbed out of the car and walked past without uttering a word. Elliot looked at the three overcrowded cars and watched as people filed out one by one. He was amazed at how many people fit into just three cars. With difficulty, he counted again out of disbelief. Twenty-three.

Chris nudged Elliot and asked, "Are ya ready t' do this?"

Elliot looked up at the night sky again and then back at Chris. "Yeah, I'm ready." Then Elliot looked around at everyone there. It was hard to see anyone; most people were hidden behind dark shadows cast by the hoods of sweatshirts. He recognized only a few faces. Most of the faces there looked back at Elliot with contempt. It was the look that most of the fighters carried around with them. He knew that most of the guys were not there on his behalf. And he knew that even though they were friends with Chris and the other guys from Brookwood, they weren't there on their behalf, either. Most of these guys had heard there was going to be a big fight and wanted in on it, and that was the only reason. Elliot would not have been surprised if only half of the guys there even knew who they were going to fight or why.

The night was hot and humid, and Elliot could smell the dew on the grass. He noticed that the ground had once been asphalt and had almost completely given way to erosion. It was now nothing more than weeds and grass trying desperately to survive in the hard, rocky ground that was left. And he couldn't help but notice the loud chirping and singing of crickets and other unfamiliar insects. *What a peaceful place. It would be cool to come here alone and have tea or something. Or bring a date.* For a moment, his mind wandered to Briseis, but he quickly shook off those thoughts. Looking around toward the cars, he saw that everyone had broken into small groups and was sitting on or standing around the cars and chatting. Of the faces he could see, he observed they had that hungry look that fighters get. Not the normal, everyday look but the more intense one—the one they get just before a fight. He knew that the shadow-covered faces had the look as well.

Elliot decided to explore a little while they waited. He headed over to the little old building behind their cars. As he approached, the insects ceased their symphony in silent protest of his intrusion. The weeds had gotten taller than those in the eroded asphalt area where they'd parked. And though he was out of sight of the cars and their streaming headlights, he could see clearly. In fact, he could see even better because he was away from the lights of the cars, and the lights of the cars were polluting the light of the moon and stars.

He looked around and noticed a tall section of rusty chain-link fence over to his right. Continuing on toward the back side of the building, he noticed another tall rusty section of chain-link fence. When he turned the corner, he came face to face with a large group of dark-hooded figures looking right at him. Elliot was stunned and just stood there for a moment, paralyzed at the intimidating dark shapes. The shadowy figures just stared at him without speaking or moving. Elliot could not see their faces but knew that their looks were not welcoming. And once again, Elliot came to terms with the fact that they might be there to fight on his side but were not there *for* him.

Trying to appear casual and unafraid, Elliot sought out Chris for the sole purpose of not being alone. "Hey Chris, what's up?"

"Oh, hey Elliot. What's goin' on?"

"Not much. Just kinda checking the place out. What is this place anyways?"

"You can't tell? It used t' be baseball diamonds. That building's an old concession stand."

Elliot felt very stupid for not recognizing what the sections of fence were for.

"There used t' be a small town around here. It had a grain silo or some kinda shit, where all the farmers brought their grain at the end of the season. Sorta like a collective or somethin'. Shit, I don't know; it had somethin' to do with farming. Anyway, the town had a small school, a church, and, like, a market. Well, the grain place went outta business, and some grain corporation bought up all the land. Most of the farmers moved or died, and their surviving families moved away. The school closed, and the church burned down, and that was the end of the little town. The corporation bought up most of the houses for more cornfields. I'm surprised they never got these old diamonds."

"How do you know so much about this place?"

"Well, I'm from here. My family got out when I was real young. Coincidentally, when I got older and after the town was gone, I discovered that punk kids, straight-edge kids, Nazis, and even ghetto thugs hung out here—a lot of party-ing, but mostly fightin'. They all fought each other: punks and skins, skins and straight-edge, gangs and gangs. Sometimes rednecks would come out here, and they always came in big numbers and would catch a smaller group of punks, skins, or straight-edge. Every once in a while, someone would bring the skins and punks and straight-edge kids together, and they would all fuck up a bunch of hicks." Chris zoned out for a moment, and Elliot knew he was reliving some of those experiences.

"Yeah, this was a great place. There's even been fights here, like organized, no-holds-barred fights. The gang-sters have all but ruined it, though. They deal drugs here, and their fights usually end up with someone bein' shot, and the cops aren't as dismissive 'bout that. They've really cracked down on people hangin' out here the past few years, but every once in a while, somethin' like this will happ'n."

Just then, Marvin walked up and said, "All right boys, ya' ready t' do this?" Elliot wondered how Marvin could have no clue as to what was going on and wondered about the suffer-ing of ignorance—about his own ignorance. Marvin showed no signs of suspicion. With as many people aware of the treacherous plot against Marvin and no one telling him, it was apparent to Elliot that no one liked the perfidious man. Just then, someone Elliot didn't know approached out of the dark and asked, "Why do we have guys hiding behind the concession house again?"

Chris impatiently replied, "I done told all you guys. We want them t' think this is going t' be a fair fight between Marv and their man Benny. They think we hate Marv and that we're lettin' 'im get his ass kicked. If they see a large group of dudes standin' around, larger than theirs, lookin' ready to fight, they might catch on t' the fact we're gonna jump their asses. Then they might leave or not even stop. If they see just three cars and a few guys, they won't think anything about it." Chris gave the guy and Elliot a long confirming look that would have made Marvin suspicious if he weren't too arrogant to see it. Benny was the alpha male in the lynching of Elliot.

Suddenly, the night grew very still and quite. Everyone around was poised dead silent, like a wild animal that sensed danger nearby. Slowly, they could hear the muffled grinding of weed-covered gravel beneath tires and see the faint hint of light coming up the lane. The sudden reality of the situation made Elliot feel very far from home, and the feeling was almost overwhelming. Three cars and a van pulled up across from their vehicles. Elliot, Chris, and a select few of their party lined up in front of their cars. Benny's crew filed out and lined up across from them in front of their own vehicles. In the small arena of lights, both crews stood for a few moments, sizing each other up before anyone spoke. Elliot didn't count Benny's crew but could tell that, despite the fact that they rode in more vehicles, they numbered about the same as his party. Nonetheless, Benny's crew seemed quite a bit larger than theirs, considering nearly half of their party was hiding behind the old crumbling building.

Benny stepped forward and said, "You ready to do this?" The man was average size, with an unnaturally defined hairline despite the close shave of his hair. His eyes appeared deep and dark, almost empty; his facial features were sharp; and his muscle definition was sharper, cutting through the tight T-shirt he was wearing. The young man stood in contrast to everyone else there. It seemed as if everyone was wearing large hooded sweatshirts draped low over their eyes and cargo shorts or loose jeans. Elliot was, too. He did not feel comfortable wearing clothes like this but was afraid that if he didn't, he would stand out or not look like a fighter.

Both lines of men were spread out across from each other like two small armies in phalanx battle formation, and Marvin stood in the center of theirs with Chris and the rest of the Brookwood Fight Club. Elliot was very close to them, and the tension was gripping him tightly. He had a bad feeling—not just because he felt that things would go badly, but deep down, he felt sorry for Marvin, and he couldn't figure out why. By all accountability, the man deserved to be punished. Elliot kept telling himself that Marvin was a liar and a backstabber and that he deserved what was coming to him. But the closer the moment got, the harder it was to convince himself that what was about to happen was justified.

Benny stepped forward a little more, which prompted the hesitant Marvin to do the same. Although Marvin wore the same hoodie-and-cargo-shorts battle dress that everyone else wore, his attire did not have the same intimidating affect. The baggy clothes that draped over his body did nothing to hide his scrawny frame. Marvin didn't step out to the center as far as Benny did. He inched forward a little and arrogantly spoke. "Son, you don't know how bad y'all fucked up! I should be askin' *you* if *you're* ready!"

Suddenly, someone pushed Marvin hard from behind, and the unsuspecting man stumbled toward Benny. Benny struck Marvin hard in the face, and Marvin fell to the ground even harder. He groaned loudly before slowly rolling over to his hands and knees. He looked up toward Chris and began uttering as if he could barely speak. "Now, guys...uhh...what... what are ya waitin' for?" His face was shockingly bloody. Blood was splattered on his face as if it had exploded out of his nose and busted lips. There was a deafening silence after he spoke, and Elliot could see the arrogance drain from his face like the blood that was now soaking the ground. Then

Marvin looked at Elliot. The look on his face was that of sheer panic and fear. For a moment, the man no longer looked like Marvin to Elliot. It seemed a familiar face, but Elliot quickly dismissed it in the fleeting moment, and all that remained was a broken man with a look of terror in his eyes.

Marvin sat up on his knees and covered his bloody mouth with one hand and reached out toward Elliot with the other. Marvin didn't say anything, but Elliot could sense his plea, his begging. It was that look that broke Elliot. The broken-down man reminded Elliot of himself: weak and afraid.

All of Elliot's sympathy for Marvin momentarily vanished, and he could only remember the first time Marvin came begging for help. And in his blinding fury, Elliot stepped forward and shouted, "Fuck you, Marvin! Where the fuck were you when these guys jumped me? Huh! When you came begging me for help. You! Who were supposed to be my friend but was using me the whole time! Fuck you, Marvin! Now I get to watch you get stomped!" Although Elliot said these words with convincing hostility, deep down he could still feel compassion pulling at him. Marvin groaned quietly, put his face in his hands, bent over and pressed it against the ground.

Suddenly, Benny's crew pounced on Marvin, stomping, kicking, and punching. There were more bodies than there was room for them to strike. Guys were trying to strike over and through the flailing arms and legs, grabbing and pulling. Marvin's moans and whimpers were barely audible over the sounds of smacking fists and the thuds of kicks and stomps. Even the moans seemed familiar to Elliot. The lynching was more shocking than Elliot had imagined, and he wondered if this was what it looked like when he was being beaten.

Elliot's forced hostility quickly drained away, and again he was flooded with sorrow. No matter how much he hated Marvin, and no matter how much Marvin deserved it, he felt overwhelming sorrow for the poor man. Although it had only been a few moments, the beating seemed to go on and on. Elliot was unaware, but Chris was watching him and knew that Elliot was faltering. And as frustrated as it made Chris, out of compassion for Elliot, he blew the whistle, the signal for their attack.

Although the moment was short, it seemed like an eternity to Elliot. Everyone on both sides froze like deer caught in the headlights of all the cars around them; it was as if someone had taken a snapshot, a picture in time. Then it was total chaos. Everyone from the Brookwood side exploded into action. Elliot stood there, still frozen, unable to comprehend what he was witnessing. There were so many arms and fists swinging, and everyone was so tangled up, he could not tell who was who. He could see splatters of something occasionally shooting in the air but, in his stupor, he did not realize that it was blood. Then Elliot hit the ground hard. He felt like he had been hit by a car, and he suddenly felt feet and fists coming down on him. The shock he felt at the ensuing chaos left him stunned, and all he could do was cover up and protect his face. "Get off of him! Get the fuck off! He's with us!" And Elliot felt arms wrap around him from behind and pull him through and away from the stomps and punches. The car that had hit Elliot was the group of fighters waiting in ambush behind the old concession stand.

"Sorry, we didn't fuckin' know!"

"Well, fuckin' pay more attention!"

"Man, fuck you!" And the hooded figure stormed away to join the raging fight.

"Man, *fuck you*!" The man who pulled Elliot to safety was Chris, who leaned over and checked his friend. Elliot was stunned by the blows he had taken to the head and more stunned by the magnitude of violence that was ensuing all around. He looked down and saw blood trickling into his lap and knew it was from his head. Then he looked up at Chris, who had a worried look on his face. "Just sit here...and don't move."

Chris turned and ran to join the fight. The riot had broken into small pockets of fights. Elliot watched as Chris ran right up to one of the small groups. Elliot did not recognize any of the men but could see that three guys were trying to subdue one large man. Two of the guys were trying to grab the larger man's arms, swinging at the larger man all the while. The third guy was staying in front of the large man, picking his shots and getting clean ones to the giant's face. But the large man was keeping his head low and protected from the two on his sides and keeping his arms free by using brute strength. And though he was taking shots to the face, he was able to keep his attackers at bay by swinging and kicking. Elliot observed a couple of unconscious bodies lying on the ground near the four fighters and wondered if the large man was responsible.

Chris ran right up behind the distracted large man and hit him hard and low to the back of the head. The man stumbled forward, and the front attacker clenched the large man around the head and started kneeing the giant in the face. The large man tried to bear hug and lift the smaller attacker, but Chris and the other two attackers grabbed the giant and began hitting, kicking, and dragging the large man to the ground. The scene reminded Elliot of a nature show he had once watched about ants and how they drag down giant wasps and spiders. When the four men got the giant down, they continued kicking and stomping the man, even after he was obviously unconscious. Elliot wondered why they needed to continue. Everywhere he looked was the same: groups of guys dragging down someone or stomping on someone who was already down.

Elliot watched one of the opposing fighters help a very bloody friend stumble back to their car before several guys ran up and pounced on the two. Then he saw two men restraining another man by the arms against one of the opposing cars. The third attacker pulled out a long, thick chain and began whipping the restrained man across the face and chest, blood splattering across the restrainers.

Hearing noise from behind him, Elliot looked back into the darkness and saw men fighting near the broken-down building. Three men were kicking and punching and trying to restrain one man who was putting up a fight. Out of nowhere, a hooded figure ran in with a large chunk of broken asphalt and smashed it into the head of one of the attackers. It made an unnerving cracking noise that sounded nothing like what he imagined a skull being cracked sounded like. In the moonlit darkness, Elliot could see blood spray into the air.

More guys came to the rescue of the restrained, and soon those who were attacking were on the defensive. Everywhere Elliot looked, he saw the same violent scene. Everyone was bloodied. Bodies littered the ground, and pools of blood soaked and weighed down the weeds that covered eroded asphalt.

"Hey! Put that away! We're not tryin' t' kill anyone!" It was Jay from Brookwood, yelling at a man who was getting a bat out of one of the vehicles. Then Elliot heard a loud thud and looked over to see a hooded man holding a limp body up to an open car door. Then the man slammed the door, and Elliot heard the thump again. It was the door smashing the limp man in the head. After the second thump, the attacker let go of the limp body, which fell between the open door and the car. The hooded figure proceeded to stomp on the lame body lying motionless at his feet.

"Hey! That's e-fucking-nough! Get off him!" Chris ran up and pushed the hooded figure, who stumbled back.

For a brief moment, it seemed like a standoff, but the hooded figure quietly said, "Man, you guys need t' light'n up." And the man ran off to stomp on another beaten soul.

"Let's get the guys together and get outta here." Elliot recognized the accent. It was Tommy calling out to Chris. Elliot could now hear whooping, hollering, glass breaking, and metal being dented. He looked across at the opposing vehicles and saw hooded figures jumping up and down on them, kicking them and throwing bricks, chunks of broken asphalt, and rocks at them. The man with the bat was smashing windows.

Chris came and helped Elliot to his feet, and they went to their car. Some of the members of the Brookwood Fight Club were limping or holding their sides, heads, or other damaged parts of their bodies. They were all covered in blood, and Elliot wondered how much of it was theirs, or someone else's. As they drove away, the overgrown drive swallowed the gory battle scene. Elliot watched as one of the opposing cars was set ablaze, the flames reaching bright and high into the night sky, consuming the once-visible stars.

twelve

For a man to conquer himself is the first and noblest of all victories.

—Plato

It was late morning, and Elliot found himself in a familiar place and in a familiar mood: lying motionless in a semiconscious state on his sofa. He was trying desperately not to relive the horrific images of the previous night. He had never seen or imagined that level of disregard to human life and wondered if some of the bodies that littered the ground had survived. And though he tried with all his might, he could not get the gruesome events out of his head: the gory images, the unnatural sounds of fists, chains, bricks, rocks, ground, and car doors hitting flesh and bone.

As the events that took place on the lonely distant parking lot forced their way into Elliot's head, he remembered looking at all the faces, trying to differentiate their facial features. But he was unable to then, and he certainly couldn't now. All of the faces that were supposedly there on his behalf looked the same. They were the faces of everyone he went to school with, of everyone he'd worked with, of peopled he'd trained with—of Joshawn and Marvin. The thought made Elliot feel more remorse for Marvin, because they weren't punishing Marvin in some sense of poetic justice. They were punishing

Marvin for simply being weak. They were satisfying their own sadistic desire to inflict unnecessary pain and destruction. *What makes people so cruel and ruthless, so devoid of sympathy for others?*

Elliot lay motionless, in part because he lacked motivation and desire to do anything, and in part because his head and body ached from the brief yet brutal assault that members of his own party had inflicted upon him. He had taken several kicks and stomps in that moment, which had compounded injuries he was still recovering from. His head, his broken hand, and his ribs pounded with relentless intensity. And though the stitches he had received from the lynching in front of his apartment had been removed the previous day, one of the kicks to his face had reopened the gash. They did not call Hyde, though. A couple of the other guys from the Brookwood Fight Club had relatively severe injuries as well, but no one wanted to involve the notorious fight-scene doctor. So Elliot lay on his sofa, his hair full of dry, crusty, dirty blood; his clothes covered in blood, dirt, and shoe prints; and his body aching and equally covered in blood, dirt, and bruises.

With a loud sigh, Elliot began to think about his future. *What am I going to do now? I can't fight like this. I don't even want to. The people on the scene are like everyone I've ever worked with. They don't care. They don't know me... they don't want to know me. They'd obviously hurt me as soon as talk to me. They look at me the same way any of my coworkers ever have—even some of the guys on my own team. And now I'm injured and can't fight, which means no money. I can't even get a job now. What am I going to do?*

Pound...pound...pound...

Through the wall came the muffled voice of Elliot's neighbor Drew. "Hey man, are you watch'n TV? Ya might wanna check this out."

With another loud sigh, Elliot sat up. He didn't care what was on television, but he didn't have the energy to shout back to Drew. At first he just sat there, hoping Drew would drop it, but the young man persisted. "Do ya see this? Are ya seein' this?"

Reluctantly, Elliot turned on the television.

"Welcome back. For those of you just tuning in, we're following a very late-breaking story. The fire department responded to calls about a blaze at an old abandoned baseball diamond north of the city and well outside city limits. When they arrived on the scene, they found two cars ablaze and several bodies on the ground. Tina Chang is live on the scene with an update. Tina, can you tell us any more about the gruesome scene that the fire department discovered?"

"Yes, Anderson, as I mentioned earlier, the fire department responded to calls around midnight. One firefighter described the scene as something out of a horror movie, with bodies lying on the ground and blood everywhere—splattered on the weeds and bushes. Local authorities were quickly called out. They are not ready to make an official statement yet, as they want to gather more evidence. I can tell you that there are at least four bodies. The sheriffs here say that this site, this old abandoned and secluded baseball field that was once a place of family and community gatherings, is now a hotbed of gang and drug activity. They believe that this is gang related. Authorities also say they've responded to similar scenes at this location that also produced dead bodies, but never anything of this magnitude."

"What about any injured people, survivors? You've mentioned a lot of blood on the scene. Do they expect to find more bodies?"

"As of right now, there has been no mention of survivors or injured persons. I overheard one of the detectives on the scene mention checking the local hospitals. As for more bodies, we have seen detectives walking around the area, and so far we've observed no other bodies being found. They are not letting us completely on the grounds at this time, as the whole area *is* a crime scene. The burning cars have been extinguished, and, as far as we can see, there are no bodies in the burned vehicles. The vehicles are, however, completely burned, and though the flames are out, the cars are still smoldering. We have not seen anyone attempt to look into the vehicles or the trunks of the vehicles."

"And what about identification? Have they identified any of the four victims?"

"It is unclear if any of the four bodies found at the scene have been identified. Again, authorities want to gather more information before releasing any more details or making any official statements."

"All right, Tina, thank you."

"Thank you, Anderson."

"That was Tina Chang, everybody, reporting live from a very horrifying crime scene. Stay with us; we'll be following the story as it develops, right here at News Center 47, your local news channel. We'll be right back after a short break from our sponsors."

Elliot sprang up and began charging around his apartment, completely forgetting about his pain. He had no thoughts of where he was going or what he was doing. Full of overwhelming adrenaline, his body went, and his mind followed without question. After several minutes of fast and intense pacing, his mind began to form cohesive thoughts and questions.

All night and into the morning, Elliot had kept thinking that some of the bodies lying on the ground when they left were dead. But the reality of that possibility did not hit him until it was confirmed on the news. And now his emotions erupted into a storm of confusion and panic. He was sad and angry that people had been beaten so severely and unnecessarily and that people had died. In his panic, he couldn't remember why they were even fighting.

The phone rang, and Elliot nervously answered, "Hello."

It was Chris. "Elliot! Meet us in front of your apartment. We're pullin' up right now!"

"Chris, oh my God, what's going on?"

Chris was speaking fast and was very obviously agitated. "Just meet us down in front! We're all going to Brookwood!"

"Brookwood, why? What's going on? Did you see the news?"

Losing his patience, Chris shouted, "Just fuckin' meet us in front!" and then the young man hung up the phone.

Elliot was shocked at the tone his friend had taken with him. For a moment, Elliot just stood there, holding the phone to his ear, still disbelieving everything that was going on. The phone started emitting a loud, annoying beep to signal it was off the hook, waking Elliot from his stupor. It was not until this awakening that the conflict of emotions waging in him succumbed to anger. Elliot unconsciously dropped the phone where he was standing and stormed downstairs.

Chris, Tommy, Mike, and Jay were all waiting in a car parked directly in front of his apartment building. The air was eerily still and hot, with the sun already beating down, and it was quiet. The guys seemed frozen, just staring at Elliot as he came down the stoop. Chris had that look again—that subtle look that Elliot had seen on Chris before and that he had seen more intensely on his sifu, his sihing, and Master Chin Li. *Is it the same look?* Elliot noticed that Tommy, Jay, and Mike had a look also.

The stillness in the air, the four frozen men, and the silence made the scene seem like a picture, and Elliot felt that old lapse in time he was so familiar with. It was he who broke the silence first, instigating time to take up its march again. His tone was not hostile at first; it was pleading. "What the fuck! Do you know people died?"

Chris responded in a flat monotone voice devoid of compassion. "Elliot, just get in the car. We can talk about it later. Just—"

Elliot's voice immediately turned from pleading to hostile. "No! We fuckin' killed people! People died!"

Some of the guys started mumbling to each other in the car. But Elliot only heard Chris shouting as he jumped out of the car. "What the fuck did ya think was gonna happen?" And he charged right up to Elliot, who had stopped on the sidewalk.

Chris's sudden change of tone and volume, his quick exit from the car, and the aggressive way he charged toward Elliot startled him, and for a brief moment, Elliot returned to pleading. "We weren't...we weren't supposed to kill anyone. We...we just..."

Getting closer to Elliot's face, intimidating him further, Chris replied in suppressed hostility. "We went there t' fuck people up, and we did. We—"

Elliot refocused, suppressed his fear, and pushed Chris back as he shouted, "No, we weren't there to kill anybody. We were there to beat the shit out of people! To beat the shit out of people!"

The other three men got out of the car. Tommy and Jay said, almost simultaneously, "Guys, let's keep it down. Let's take this to the clubhouse."

Mike began shouting at Elliot. "Elliot, why you bein' such a bitch? We did this for you!"

Turning to Mike, Elliot responded, "No you didn't! You did it for you! You, like everyone else, just wanted to fuck shit up! It was guys like—"

Mike cut Elliot off. "Man, fuck you! I always knew you were a punk bitch!"

Elliot, momentarily losing his temper, responded in kind. "Man, fuck you! *You're* a bitch!"

Tommy and Jay were now holding Mike back. Elliot turned back to Chris, who was just staring at him, his face hard. Again pleading, Elliot said, "Chris, man, what the fuck? I know you didn't want people to get killed. I saw you—we need to go to the police."

Immediately, Tommy, Jay, and Mike started shouting. "Man, fuck that!" yelled Tommy and Jay, while Mike shouted, "Fuck that! I *knew* he would break! I knew he was gonna bitch out!"

Chris just stared intently at Elliot, who stared back, ignoring the other three men. Then Chris spoke. "Man, listen to you. All this time makin' references t' martial arts and about bein' a warrior...actin' so fuckin' smart all the time...actin' so righteous. What did ya expect, scholar? We'd all help each other up afterward and be friends? Go buy each other a beer and be pals?"

Still pleading, Elliot tried to cut in. "Chris, this isn't—"

But Chris didn't allow it. "No! *You* listen, Mr. I-Wanna-Be-a-Warrior, this is it. This is the jung wu. This is what *you* wanted!"

Elliot was immediately surprised that Chris used the term *jung wu*, an old reference to the Chinese martial arts culture, the warrior culture. Seeing the surprised look on Elliot's face, Chris went on. "Yeah, you're not the only scholar around here. I know all about the jung wu; I've been livin' it." Chris placed emphasis on the words of this last statement and thrust his finger at Elliot with every word. "I've seen plenty of guys like you come and go, and you're all the same, thinkin' this is a Disney movie where the good guys win and the bad guys learn their lesson, and everybody's cool with each other in the end. Well, shit ain't like that!"

Chris, in his excitement, started to raise his voice back to a shout. "There are no good guys...there are no bad guys! Just a buncha guys...a buncha warriors...soldiers *without a war*! We have no great war t' fight. We don't wanna go fight for some bullshit politician! What-the-fuck-ever! We have each other, and those guys layin' back there at the diamond knew what they were doin'—what they were gettin' themselves into. They would've done the same thing. It could've been any one of us still layin' there. And I don't know 'bout you, Disney, but we all knew what we were gettin' into and how it could've turned out."

Elliot caught himself halfway agreeing with what Chris was saying. He wanted to believe that this mentality and lifestyle was righteous, that this subculture was as close to a warrior society as he was going to get. But, deep down, he felt a pull, something telling him that what they did was still not right. Elliot tried frantically to think of a good argument as to why they were wrong and what their appropriate actions should be, but he couldn't. All he could muster was,

"Chris, you're wrong...that's wrong. We need to do the right thing. We need to make this right. We need—"

Immediately Tommy, Jay, and Mike started shouting their protests again. "No fucking way" and "Fuck that" and "We're not going to the police!" All the while Chris stared at Elliot. As the three men were shouting their objections, they very subtly fanned out, almost circling Elliot. Elliot noticed a subtle change in the air. It was thicker. And everything outside the shouts of the three men grew silent, even more silent than it already was—the silence almost seemed to envelope the shouts of the three men. And suddenly, Elliot understood the look he had seen on all the important people in his life; the look that had eluded and confused him all this time. And though Elliot thought the look everyone shared was the same, there was something distinctly different about the look these four men had compared to his teachers. His teachers were full of love, compassion and understanding—their look was of recognition. These four men that stood before Elliot now, were full of anger, hate, hostility, and fear, and it showed in their look. It frightened Elliot. And now they had that animalistic look in their eyes, that hungry look, and Elliot knew what that meant too. He also knew that these men weren't his friends anymore—weren't ever his friends. He knew that these men were incapable of friendship.

"I can't tell you guys what to do, but I'm going to the police!"

* * *

Elliot walked down the hall to the back room where Master Chin Li always sat. The hall seemed longer and darker than usual. As Elliot slowly pushed open the door, he beheld the old man's back toward him, bending over in a field of wildflowers, and the soft dim light that lit the tearoom slowly brightened into a warm summer day. A gentle breeze combed the beautiful array of wildflowers that stretched as far as the eye could see. Chin Li was standing several feet in front of Elliot and moving so subtly and gracefully that it was as if the old tea master were swaying with the flowers. Elliot could hear the old man softly speaking to the flowers, and when Elliot could finally make out what the old man was saying, he realized Chin Li was quoting from *The Book of Tea*.

"Tell me, gentle flowers, teardrops of the stars, standing in the garden, nodding your heads to the bees as they sing of dews and the sunbeams, are you aware of the fearful doom that awaits you? Today my ruthless hand closes around your throats. I'll wrench you, tear you asunder, limb by limb, and bear you away from your quiet homes. I say how lovely you are while my fingers are still moist with your blood."

Chin Li held a flower up to the sun to study it more intently, with his back still to Elliot, who could barely see the flower from his vantage point. After several moments, Chin Li again spoke to the flower, still quoting *The Book of Tea*. "What were the crimes you must have committed in your last incarnation to warrant such punishment as this?" And the old man turned ever so slightly toward Elliot, barely revealing his profile, and held the flower up so the young man could see better. He spoke to Elliot: "Is this Chan?"

Suuuuuck...suuuuuck...suuuuuck...suuuuuck...suuuuuck... suuuuuck...

Elliot had a sudden image of his job at the processing plant, and it startled him to consciousness. He struggled to open his eyes to bright, penetrating light. It was as if he could not completely wake himself, as if someone were holding him asleep. His body had a profound aching that felt like he had slept way too long. As his eyes began to focus, he was momentarily confused by his surroundings but slowly recognized them as a hospital room. The noise that had frightened him from his deep slumber, the noise he had thought was his vacuum tool, was, in fact, the slow hiss of an oxygen mask strapped to his face.

"You've been out for two days." Elliot did not notice his sifu sitting close by until the man spoke. It took Elliot a moment to process what Sifu Miller had said as he continued to regain his senses and understand where he was.

Elliot wanted to ask what happened, what was going on, because he couldn't remember anything, but the breathing mask prevented him from speaking. As his senses continued to slowly return, he felt his head pounding. Then he noticed his right arm and left wrist in casts. He raised his left arm and, with the fingers protruding from the cast, felt the bandages on his head. It was difficult for him to breathe, and Elliot knew his ribs must be in the same condition as the rest of his body.

"Uh, one moment...I was told to contact the nurse if you woke." Sifu Miller left the room.

Elliot tried to think, to figure out what was going on, but the pounding in his head was making it very difficult for him to concentrate. A moment later, Sifu Miller returned. "Well, Elliot, it seems you were assaulted by a few individuals. I've spoken with the police, and they informed me that, according to your neighbor, the guys who assaulted you were, well, supposed to be some friends of yours...or so your neighbor thought. The officer said that your neighbor also told them—"

"Well, well, how are we doing?" A nurse walked briskly into the room and marched right up to Elliot's bedside, picked up his chart, and read it. Sifu Miller did not continue speaking.

Moments later, the doctor came in and checked the charts and Elliot's vital signs. He then checked the monitors before turning to Elliot and saying, "Well, I think we can remove these." The doctor turned to the nurse, who was standing by, and told her she could remove the breathing mask and catheter. Not really speaking to anyone in particular, the doctor went on. "All of his vitals are good—just where we want 'em. I'm going to order another CAT scan...probably be done in the morning. Everything is looking good. He's been improving steadily since he got here, so...I half expected him to wake soon. Obviously, he just woke, so we're gonna want to monitor him here in the ICU for at least another forty-eight hours, pending further testing." The doctor turned and faced

Sifu Miller directly. "Other than that, we'll just continue to monitor him, and the nurses will keep me posted as to any changes in condition." Then the doctor turned and walked out of the room.

Elliot raised his head forward so the nurse could remove the bands of the breathing mask from around his head. This sent a jolt of pain through his body that made him grunt loudly. "You think that hurt, wait until I remove the catheter." As the nurse proceeded to remove the catheter, Elliot tried to clench his fists and grit his teeth, but these acts proved to be nearly as painful as the removal of the long rubber tube. The pain was so intense that Elliot blacked out for a moment.

In an attempt to divert attention, Sifu Miller asked the nurse, "You're not the nurse that's been taking care of him. What happened to...the other girl? Not that it matters. I was just under the impression she'd be here all day."

The young nurse chuckled and said, "No, that's OK. You're talking about Alissa. She had a family emergency, so I'm kinda helping out over here. I usually work in the lab. My name is Victoria." And the girl pulled her name tag up and away from her chest so Sifu Miller could see it more clearly. He had not paid any attention to her when she first came into his room, as he was very confused and in pain. However, after the momentary lapse in consciousness, the intense pain brought him to full awareness, and he could not help but notice her beauty now. Victoria continued talking to Sifu Miller. "You guys are the martial arts guys, right?"

"Uh, yeah." Sifu Miller was a little surprised at this question.

Misinterpreting Sifu Miller's look, Victoria quickly said, "Oh, I'm sorry. Alissa is...she's actually a friend of mine. She knows I'm from a martial arts family, and she told me that...about you guys...at least about..." She gestured down to Elliot.

"Oh no, it's OK. I was just surprised you could tell—or how you could tell—we were martial artists. You say you're family does martial arts? Are they from around here?"

"No. I mean, yeah, my family does martial arts, well, my dad. But they're not from around here—my family. I moved here for work."

"Do you still train? What is it, what art?"

"My dad, he trains and teaches a little bit of everything. He's retired military, but when I was growing up, we moved a lot. Everywhere we went, my dad would seek out martial arts teachers, no matter what the art was, and he'd train as long as we lived there. And, of course, I had to learn also. I hated it growing up, but I started appreciating it when I got older. I trained with him until I moved here a year ago. Sooo..." With a slight shrug, Victoria continued. "I guess, to answer your question, a little bit of everything. Mostly Japanese arts—judo, karate, jujitsu, aikido...We did train a couple animal forms at one point, but not really application." And the young nurse felt suddenly awkward. Thinking she was speaking too much, she abruptly ended her reply with another slight shrug.

"Do you still train?"

"Oh yeah...well, kinda, mostly like, cardio-type stuff. Some of the drills and forms I know are very cardio, so...I don't do any application. I think about it sometimes. I mean, I like the idea of that kind of training, but mostly I'm too busy with work."

"Well, life is about balance," replied Sifu Miller.

And Elliot smiled inside at the familiarity of the lesson.

Sifu Miller continued, "Well, I'm not trying to give a sales pitch or anything, but if you're ever interested, I run a school here in town, Shaolin Academy. Look us up if you ever decide you want to start training again or take your training in that direction."

"I'll do that. And is this one of your students?" The nurse gestured toward Elliot again.

"Uh, yes, he is." Not knowing what to say and not wanting to go into why Elliot was in the condition he was in, Sifu Miller said no more.

The nurse gave Elliot a quick and subtle look-over and a peculiar smile that both Elliot and Sifu Miller noticed. She turned back to Sifu Miller. "OK, well, if you or he need anything, just press the call button, and I or someone else will be right in." Looking back to Elliot, Victoria said, "If you need to use the bathroom, you can also press the call button." Looking back to Sifu Miller, she finished, "I'll be back to check in on him in a bit." Then she walked out.

Sifu Miller just stared at Elliot for a moment. Elliot was sure he could see hints of a wry grin. Sifu Miller picked up where he had left off before the young nurse had come in. "As I was saying, your neighbor told police that you were jumped by a different group of guys a couple of weeks ago. The doctor here says you look like you had previous serious injuries from what looks like a beating from that time frame, so it's safe to at least assume your neighbor is telling the truth about a previous assault. He also says you have scars from lacerations in different stages of healing that go back several weeks or more." Sifu Miller paused for a moment before going on. "Which means you've been stitched up a few different times over the past couple of months, not counting this time."

Elliot's headache was still making it difficult for him to process thoughts. There was a long silence between the two men before Elliot finally spoke. "Sifu, I don't know...I can't remember much, just bits and pieces. I do know that you were right. Those people...all they want to do is hurt others..."

Elliot suddenly saw images of bodies lying on the ground and did something he used to do all too often but hadn't done in a long time: he started to weep. Except this time, he did not weep for himself, but for the others. Trying to hold back the tears, he went on. "To kill people." There was another short silence before Elliot continued. "And I helped 'em. Sifu, I fucked up. What am I gonna do?" Elliot couldn't hold back the sobs.

After a moment, Sifu Miller spoke. "I don't believe you helped kill anybody. I don't even know the whole story, but I know you're no killer."

Elliot shouted, "It was my idea—*mine*!" And he sat up and hit himself in his chest a few times as if to emphasize his incrimination. Ignoring the pain he inflicted on himself, Elliot continued. "It was my idea to trick people, to deceive people, into coming—to set people up to get beat down. *Mine*!" And in his torment, the broken young man fell back into his bed.

Again Sifu Miller spoke softly. "Look, Elliot, I'm not going to say you didn't make mistakes...make bad choices. You did. And you're going to have to live with those choices. You lost control of your emotions and made bad decisions. What's done is done. You can't change that; you can't go back. You can only use your experiences to help make better decisions right now. Mistakes...they're opportunities...opportunities to grow and learn, opportunities to do right. Elliot, get control of your emotions. Figure out what the right thing to do is *right now*, and do it!"

The battered young man's sobs softened. "But, Sifu, I don't know what to do. People are dead, and I feel like it's my fault. Tell me what to do."

"Elliot, I can't tell you what to do or what you need to do. You need to figure that out. Find the courage and figure that out yourself. As for those who died, that's not your fault. You didn't make them show up to illegal violent activities or whatever. They came on their own. They made their own bad choices."

"But they were there because of me, because of my idea. I set them up!"

Sifu Miller gave a slight shrug. "I'm not telling you not to feel bad. You're right; people died an unnecessary death. But I would encourage you to feel bad for them whether you were involved or not. Because it's sad to see anyone die, especially an unnecessary death. But the path they were on...they would have showed up anyway. Whether it was something you planned or some other violent encounter that someone else planned. They're on the fighter's path, not the warrior's path. They want to conquer each other. If they're not conquering others, they're being conquered by others, and that's what happened. That's it; it's that simple. And it's really out of your hands. All you can do is learn from their deaths and your experience in the world of fighters. Let their deaths be wasted on all the fighters out there, but don't let their deaths be wasted on you."

Both men fell silent for a long time. Elliot knew his sifu was right. Even if there were any doubt, Elliot had learned the hard way to trust his sifu. He wanted to again ask his sifu what he should do, how he should make things right, or, at the very least, how to make things better. Elliot was confident that his sifu would know exactly what to do. But he knew that his sifu would not give him the answer. His sifu would continue to insist that he figure it out himself; that he overcome his fear, sorrow, insecurities, self-doubt, and self-pity; and that he find the strength and wisdom himself.

The hospital room was silent, save for the electrical hum of medical equipment and the air vents blowing out a gentle but cold breeze. Finally, Elliot sat up and said, "I think I'd like to go to the restroom."

"Let me call the nurse."

"No, I'd really like to just do it myself."

Sifu Miller started to protest and insist, but Elliot stopped him.

"Sifu, it's OK. I can do this, I can. I need to...I want a minute...I need a minute to myself. I can do it."

"I'll just step out. You can use the bedpan and have some time to yourself."

"No, Sifu, really...I'll just walk to the restroom."

Sifu Miller said, "Wait just a minute" and walked out of the room. Moments later, he returned with a walker. Elliot did not care to ask how or where his sifu got the walker. Sifu Miller helped Elliot sit up and then stand up before placing the walker directly in front of his battered body. Getting up proved to be excruciating to Elliot, but he suppressed all of his grunts and controlled his body so as not to jerk. Sifu Miller held on to Elliot as the young man started stepping, but Elliot stopped and simply said, "You know, Sifu, thanks for helping me get up. I don't think I could've without you. But I can manage from here. I can."

Sifu Miller let go of his grip and stood there as his student scooted slowly away. "OK, I'm going to just step out for a little bit. I'll be back in a little while." And the teacher stood there, staring at Elliot with a look of pride that his student did not turn around to see.

"OK." As Elliot walked slowly and with great effort to the small bathroom adjacent to his bed, pain consumed his entire body. It was difficult to use the walker, as his right arm was in a 90-degree cast with the bend at the elbow, forcing him to get uncomfortably low on his right side to reach the walker, compounding the pain in his body. The cast on his left wrist was only from the elbow down, so he could bend his elbow, but the cast covered most of his hand, and he could not grip the walker correctly. He could only put his weight in the palm of the cast, creating a pressure that sent shock waves of pain through his broken hand and wrist every time he took a step. His legs and torso hurt so bad that every time he let his weight down on his feet, he thought he was going to fall. But he persisted.

When he finally trekked the short distance into the bathroom, he stopped and looked at himself in the mirror. For a moment, he didn't recognize himself, and it surprised him so much that he briefly forgot about his pain. It was not the swelling, bruises, or bandages that made him unrecognizable to himself. It was something different. And it took him a while to figure out what it was. Then, finally, it hit him: the look. He had the look that he had seen on his sifu, his sihings, and Master Chin Li so many times before. That look...

After staring at himself for several moments and finishing in the bathroom, Elliot began the arduous journey back to his bed. With his head down and in full concentration,

Elliot did not notice his friend Master Chin Li standing in is way until he about bumped into the old man. Startled, Elliot looked up and saw surprise in the wise old tea master's face. After a moment's pause, the tea master took a small step back, bowed deeply, and said, "Ah, now you a'e t'ue wa'io', Maste' Elliot."

www.ingramcontent.com/pod-product-compliance
Lightning Source LLC
Chambersburg PA
CBHW030250130626
46549CB00002B/465